THE POWER OF CROSS

Anthony Agbonkhese

Copyright © 2024 by Anthony Agbonkhese

ISBN: 978-1-960764-75-1 (sc)
ISBN: 978-1-960764-76-8 (hc)
ISBN: 978-1-960764-77-5 (eBook)

All rights reserved. No part of this publication may be reproduced, distributed, or transmitted in any form or by any means, including photocopying, recording, or other electronic or mechanical methods, without the prior written permission of the author, except in the case of brief quotations embodied in critical reviews and certain other non-commercial uses permitted by copyright law.

www.writeandreleasepublishing.com

Table of Contents

Chapter 1 God and Adam Breath of Life 1

Chapter 2 The Temple Of God: Knowledge of Good and Evil 7

Chapter 3 Light and Darkness Christ Mind and Carnal Mind ... 21

Chapter 4 God Blessed Adam and Eve 25

Chapter 5 The Tree of Life Return of the Prodigal Son 32

Chapter 6 The Power of the Cross 39

Chapter 7 The Maker's Eye 46

Chapter 8 God Throws Away The Bad Fruits 57

Chapter 9 Climb Up To God 59

Chapter 10 Baptism of the Soul 62

Chapter 11 Cover the Grave the Enemy Dug 68

Chapter 12 The Art of Healing 72

Chapter 13 Christ Laborers 77

Chapter 14 Songs and Prayers 83

Chapter 1
GOD AND ADAM BREATH OF LIFE

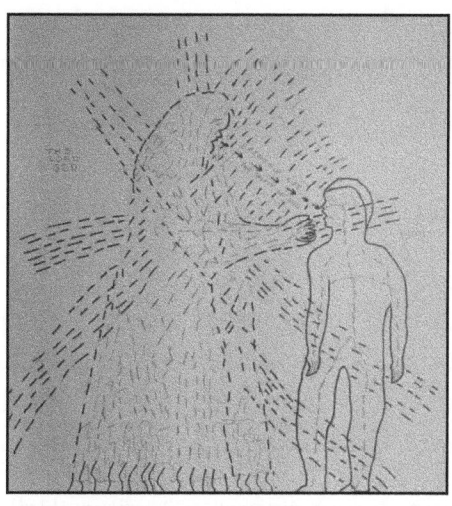

Every living thing has a physical, spiritual, and divine nature. God made it so. He created heaven and this physical paradise, earth, and placed us here. Since the beginning, humans have been thinking and asking about the source and origin of things: the mystery of life, the divine, the spiritual, and the physical; the higher source above and beyond—stars, the sun, the moon, the earth, days, nights, water, wind, fire, air, rain, mountains, caves, trees, fruits, seeds, herbs, food, and everything that lives and grows on planet earth. The creatures of the sea, air, and land are wonderful, mysterious, diverse, scientific, beautiful, wise, unique, small and large, balanced, and complete. Man begins to observe, ponder, and study all these things around us—what they are, how they work, and how they live. They want to know who created them and who made them.

God the Creator is a spirit, and being spiritual, He created all physical things and gave them life. Adam and Eve, the work of God, possess both physical and divine aspects, seen and unseen; they lived and occupied the physical earth. Within them were the Holy Spirit of God and the human soul.

God the Creator is a spirit, and being spiritual, he created all the physical things and gave them life. Adam and Eve, the work of God, have physical and divine aspects seen and unseen; they lived and occupied the physical earth. In them were the Holy Spirit of God and the human soul.

Humans continue to pray and meditate, seeking the Creator day and night. Then their minds, consciousness, and sense of awareness begin to open, and they find God. They discover the Holy Spirit and the soul that lives inside every person. God begins to teach them.

Ideals, formulas, theories, and principles for doing things begin to increase. Soon, the Creator sends prophets and messengers to teach them about God, to love one another, and to help them understand the origin of things, the science behind creation, and its principles.

At the beginning, group reverence, territorial tribal wars, wildlife, sickness, and natural disasters posed a threat to humans. Did humans evolve, transforming from primates? Has the transformation and evolution stopped? The primates still exist. Where are the newly transformed humans? Early humans were unique but primitive in their thoughts and ways of doing things.

As humans pray, they grow closer to the Creator, and divine intervention, creativity, and advancement begin to emerge. To navigate these confrontations, the Spirit of God reveals to them how to make tools and weapons, understand the laws of nature, grasp principles and science, and appreciate the value of natural resources that have led to modern technology and development. Wildlife no longer threatens us; we threaten them."

"They are afraid of humans; they are running out of places to live, and they are going extinct.

Now we know who God the Father is. He has visited us as a human, and we saw Him in person. We are the children of God the Father, but the mystery of the Father and all of creation remains. Children are inquisitive; they question, "Where did God the Father originate from? Where is He taking us?"

Behold, the man has become as one of us to know good and evil now, lest he put forth his hand and take also of the tree of life and eat and live forever. (Genesis 3:22) The Holy Spirit is the tree of life, which the soul will have to climb to arise to and return to the Creator. God the Father is taking us toward a better future; he leads, and we follow.

"God said, let us make man in our image, after our likeness. God created man in his own image; in the image of God created he him, male and female." (Genesis 1:26–27)

In today's technology, through 3D dimensions and electronic drafting, we create the blueprint of the product that needs to be produced. The Lord God created the blueprint, the divine and physical aspects of Adam and Eve, the breath of God to be reproduced in the world of form (earth), and kept them in the Garden of Eden.

The Lord God commanded the man, saying, "Of every tree of the garden thou mayest freely eat; but of the tree of knowledge of good and evil thou shalt not eat of it, for in the day that thou eatest thereof thou shalt surely die." The serpent is among the creatures the Lord God made.

Adam and Eve were in the presence of the Lord God and also in the presence of the serpent. Now the serpent was more subtle than any beast of the field which the Lord God had made. And he said unto the woman, "Yea, hath God said, ye shall not eat of every tree of the garden?" And the woman said unto the serpent, "We may eat of the fruit of the trees of the garden; but of the fruit of the tree…"

And the Lord God formed man from the dust of the ground and breathed into his nostrils the breath of life, the spirit of God. (Genesis 2:7)

Through the breath of God, the image of God, man became a living soul. Judas came to the garden, guiding a detachment of soldiers and some officials from the chief priests and the Pharisees. They were carrying torches, lanterns, and weapons. Jesus, knowing all that was going to happen to him, went out and asked them, "Who is it you want?" "Jesus of Nazareth," they replied. "I am he," Jesus said. For the second time, "I am he." They drew back and fell to the ground. (John 18:3–6)

Let's pay attention to these three words: God, he, and him. First, God the Father is the Creator. Second, God the Son is he who comes from God, the divine working energy of the invisible God, the firstborn of God. On the third day, he was raised from the dead by God the Father, and he appeared to Mary Magdalene and to the apostles. Third is the Holy Spirit, the divine male child. "Whosoever shall receive one of these little ones receives me, and who receives me receives the Father that sent me" (Mark 9:37).

"And their angel always beholds the face of my Father who is in heaven" (Matthew 18:10).

"Fourth, the soul is the perfect image of God and the animating principle of humans. Fifth is the human spirit, which represents human energy. Sixth are the human senses. Seventh is the physical human, the visible aspect of God."

"Every tree of the garden," and the woman said to the serpent, "We may eat the fruit of the trees of the garden, but of the fruit of the tree which is in the midst of the garden, God has said, "You shall not eat of it, neither shall you touch it, lest you die."

I made minor adjustments for consistency and clarity.

And the serpent said unto the woman, "Ye shall not surely die. For God doth know that in the day ye eat thereof, your eyes shall be opened, and ye shall be as gods, knowing good and evil."

And when the woman saw that the tree was good for food, and that it was pleasant to the eyes, and a tree to be desired to make one wise, she took of the fruit thereof and did eat, and gave also unto her husband with her, and he did eat. And the eyes of them both were opened, and they knew that they were naked; and they sewed fig leaves together and made themselves aprons.

And they heard the voice of the Lord God walking in the garden in the cool of the day, and Adam and his wife hid themselves from the presence of the Lord God among the trees. "Where art thou?" And he said, "I heard thy voice in the garden, and I was afraid because I was naked; and I hid myself." And he said, "Who told thee that thou wast naked? Hast thou eaten of the tree whereof I commanded thee that thou should not eat?" And the man said, "The woman whom thou gavest to be with me, she gave me of the tree, and I did eat." And the Lord God said unto the woman, "What is this that thou hast done?" And the woman said, "The serpent beguiled me, and I did eat."

And the Lord God said unto the serpent, "Because thou hast done this, thou art cursed above all cattle, and above every beast of the field; upon thy belly shalt thou go, and dust shalt thou eat all the days of thy life. And I will put enmity between thee and the woman, and between thy seed and her seed; it shall bruise thy head, and thou shalt bruise his heel."

Unto the woman He said, "I will greatly multiply thy sorrow and thy conception; in sorrow thou shalt bring forth children, and thy desire shall be to thy husband, and he shall rule over thee." And unto Adam He said, "Because thou hast hearkened unto the voice of thy wife and hast eaten of the tree, of which I commanded thee, saying, "Thou shalt not eat of it: cursed is the ground for thy sake; in sorrow shalt thou eat of it all the days of thy life. Thorns also and thistles shall it bring forth to thee; and thou shalt eat the herb of the field. In the sweat of thy face shalt thou eat bread, till thou return unto the ground; for out of it wast thou taken: for dust thou art, and unto dust shalt thou return."

And Adam called his wife's name Eve because she was the mother of all living. Unto Adam also and to his wife did the Lord God make coats of skins and clothed them. And the Lord God said, "Behold, the man has become as one of us to know good and evil; now, lest he put forth his hand and take also of the tree of life, and eat, and live forever."

Therefore, the Lord God sent him forth from the Garden of Eden to till the ground from whence he was taken. So He drove out the man and placed at the east of the Garden of Eden Cherubim and a flaming sword which turned every way to keep the way of the tree of life.

Some people will say that for Adam and Eve, it was fine since they were the beginning of human beings. First, they were immortal and lived in heaven in the presence of God the Father, but then they were sent to earth to be mortal beings for eating the forbidden fruit. From the beginning, they were with God and did not have the knowledge of good and evil. It all happened after they ate the forbidden fruit, and they passed the knowledge on to us from generation to generation.

What is this fruit that they ate, and what is the knowledge of good and evil that they gained? Adam blamed God, saying, "The woman whom Thou gave to be with me, she gave me of the tree," and they became afraid after eating the forbidden fruit. Eve blamed the serpent. They ate the fruit of the knowledge of good and evil; their eyes were opened, and they knew that they were naked. They could see as humans and think as humans.

The forbidden fruit represents a spiritual separation from God. As humans, we are partly God and partly human, and the power of God is within us. How we handle this power is what matters for bringing forth either goodness, joy, peace, and love, or anger, hatred, and destruction. When we obey, we come closer to God; when we disobey, we separate further away.

Chapter 2

THE TEMPLE OF GOD: KNOWLEDGE OF GOOD AND EVIL

And so it is written, the first man, Adam, was made a living soul; the last Adam, Jesus Christ, was made a quickening spirit. How is it that the first was not spiritual but that which is natural, and afterward that which is spiritual? (1 Corinthians 15:45-46) The first man is of the earth, earthy; the second man is the Lord from above, a heavenly, life-giving spirit.

Make alive the first man with the knowledge of good and evil—God consciousness and human consciousness in us. In the book of Genesis, on the sixth day, God created land animals and humans. Adam and Eve were made with the breath of God and the soil of the earth, and they became living souls. On the seventh day, God rested from His work of creation.

The breath of God encompasses all the aspects of God: the Father, the Son, and the Holy Spirit. The flesh was made from the soil of the earth and became alive and active with the breath of God.

There are two spirits: the Holy Spirit of God and the human spirit. There are two minds in every human: the Christ mind (the Holy Spirit) and the carnal mind (the fleshly human spirit). To do well is the will of the Holy Spirit of God. To do evil is the will of the human spirit in the flesh; it was the serpent that deceived Adam and Eve and caused them to sin.

God the Creator sent His first Son, Jesus Christ, to come and save humanity. While on earth, He obeyed God and disobeyed the devil. Because God was pleased with Him, He has forgiven us of the sins that were passed on to us from Adam and Eve.

Humans have different religions, beliefs, and interpretations, but the same mind: love and hate, obey and disobey, preserve and destroy, peace and anger.

We humans don't completely know why we are able to do the things that we do. God knows; He made us and understands the spirit of God and the spirit of humans.

The Trinity: God the Father, God the Son, and God the Holy Spirit. In the Bible, Lucifer was a high-ranking angel. He rebelled against God, was defeated, lost his post in heaven, and was sent down to earth. Did he think that humans did not deserve mercy and forgiveness, or did he believe he was the one to rule heaven and earth? He did not create heaven and earth; God the Father did.

God has sent prophets, but they could not take away sins from humanity forever, nor could Lucifer if he was sent. He and his angels, with their angelic power, incarnated as humans and dwell among us.

Your body is the temple of God; the Holy Spirit of God dwells in us. We worship God because He lives in you. The evil one has no power over me; he has two options: to go away from me or to die by the rod and staff of God.

God the Father loves us greatly and would do anything to protect us from every evil, keeping us alive, safe, and happy. For this, Jesus came into the world as a human; He sacrificed Himself for us and shared His flesh and blood for the forgiveness of our sins.

Before Adam and Eve, God the Father and God the Son existed; there was no Adam and Eve. God made man in His own image. God took the soil of the earth, molded Adam, and breathed into his nostrils the breath of life; Adam became a living soul. Jesus Christ is the first Son of God. Adam is His brother, the second son of God. Adam was lonely, and the Lord God made him a companion, Eve.

God placed them on earth to replenish the earth, to learn, discover, and look after the things that He created. They lived on earth and in heaven together with God the Father and God the Son. Adam and Eve disobeyed God by eating the forbidden fruit, and they were driven out of heaven down to earth.

God the Creator remained in them through the Holy Spirit: the Trinity—God the Father, God the Son, and God the Holy Spirit. God the Father is in God the Son, God the Son is in God the Holy Spirit, and God the Holy Spirit is in the human soul. The human soul is with the human spirit. Adam and Eve were not born of humans; they were made in heaven by God the Father through the Son. They were divine and spiritual in nature and lived in the Garden of Eden, the divine earth.

God did not send them down to the physical earth from the beginning; they were a divine blueprint and would not function as humans but as angels—divine beings with no flesh, no death, and with the power to go to and from earth. Their work was to tend the earth, multiply, learn, and discover. For them to function on earth, there needed to be a combination of the spiritual and the physical, the heavenly being and the earthly being.

The Lord God took the soil of the physical earth, molded it, and made clay to form; they received the breath of God. Adam and Eve became living souls. Adam and Eve were the first from God on earth. Cain and Abel were the first real humans to live on the planet. God provided for Adam and Eve and watched them grow more divine and less human.

They fell to earth from heaven after God had sent them out of the Garden of Eden. God said, "I will not leave you as orphans. I will return to you." At the beginning, all they knew was their Father, the Lord God; but as they grew, so did their human minds, sense of awareness, and fascination with all things around them.

In the image of God, He created them male and female. Everything He has made: behold, it was very good. In Isaiah, God said…

My thoughts are not your thoughts, neither are your ways my ways. For as the heavens are higher than the earth, so are my ways higher than your ways. For as the rain comes down, and the snow from heaven, and does not return there, but waters the earth, and makes it bring forth and bud, that it may give seed to the sower and bread to the eater, so shall my word be that goes forth out of my mouth; it shall not return to me void, but it shall accomplish that which I please, and it shall prosper in the thing whereunto I sent it.

God is the Creator of all things, the Alpha and the Omega, King of kings, Lord of lords, God of gods, Prince of princes, the source and destination, the beginning and the ending, the finite and the infinite, the omni-Creator, omnipresent, omnipotent, omnidirectional, omni-Granter, omni-vision, omni-hearing, omni-reach, omni-Healer, and omni-Protector. His ways and His thoughts are beyond human comprehension; He makes, creates, preserves, destroys, and restores. Father God and Mother God are the beginning and the end, and in the middle are the children.

From the past to the present, He has revealed knowledge to us through His prophets and messengers, from the Bible, from dreams and visions, and through thoughts and meditation, which have directed us to where we need to be. Knowledge and direction from God have guarded us and enabled us to think and do things in the past and present, preparing us for the future.

"The tree of the knowledge of good and evil is human—Adam and Eve. Behold, mankind has become as one of us to know good and evil" (Genesis 3:22).

God was pleased with Abel's offering but was not pleased with Cain's offering. Abel offered the best of his produce to God, while ordinary Cain offered any of his produce to God. If you do well, you will be accepted; and if you do not do well, you will not be accepted. You will get angry.

The desire to commit sin is waiting. You will be tempted. Stay with the Holy Spirit, say no to the devil, be in control, and he will walk away from you. Jesus Christ prayed, "Not my will but the will of God be done on earth as it is done in heaven."

Adam and Eve were created perfect, with two minds: God's mind and the human mind, and two spirits: God's spirit and the human spirit. They disobeyed God, moved away from His presence, and debased the energy of God within them. They became more human and less divine, corrupt in the sight of God. He sent them out of the Garden of Eden.

What is this fruit that the serpent gave to Adam and Eve that altered their minds? Humans desire and need charm, attraction, seduction, gravity, stimulation, and the emanation of energy inside and outside. The Christ mind is the will of God, and the carnal mind is the will of the flesh.

The spirit of God is willing to do the will of God, but the human spirit is weak and willing to do the will of the flesh. The flesh is weak due to wants and needs, attraction, and consumption of worldly things. Worldly things are good; they are gifts from God and from humans. We need them, but acquiring them through evil means is wrong.

God is a spirit; the devil is also a spirit, but a lesser spirit. Good and evil are competing within us. The human spirit is a lesser spirit, competing with the higher spirit of God. The children of this world are not wiser than the children of light.

God led the Israelites out of Egypt. Jesus Christ was born in Bethlehem, Israel, the chosen one. We all have the Christ mind and the carnal mind. Naturally, with God-given talent and energy, we work hard to acquire the things we need, and in certain cases, we call on God's power for supernatural and divine intervention.

No one is completely holy and perfect except God, and we should acknowledge this and stop acting perfect or seeking perfection from others. In either case, we are all children of God. Jesus died on the cross to set us all free from our sins.

All we have to do is believe in God and also believe in the Son of God, Jesus Christ. Beware of the serpent and be peaceful as a dove. The dove represents the spirit of God, while the serpent represents the human spirit, both of which exist in us all. Who you are and your actions determine whether you are a dove or a serpent.

The dove is a peaceful and harmless spirit of God, the Maker and Creator of all things seen and unseen; He does not fear anything, for He created all things. The serpent, representing the human spirit, is crafty and elusive. Many expressions and interpretations can be attached to the dove and serpent.

Humans naturally behave as they do, but our wants and needs affect our attitudes, feelings, and actions. Adam and Eve did not commit evil; they disobeyed God, left His divine presence, and obeyed the serpent. He led them to the tree of the knowledge of good and evil, persuaded them, and they ate of it, acquiring the knowledge of good and evil and death.

Jesus Christ prayed, "Let your will be done, not mine." God made us, and doing things His way is better. Had they taken one step further, they would have found the tree of life, eaten from it, and lived forever.

Cain was the first human to obey the devil; he committed evil and murdered his brother, Abel. Be peaceful as a dove and wise as a serpent. The dove should be wise as the serpent, and the serpent should be peaceful as a dove and learn from the spirit of God.

Our body is a composition of all things, including the dove and the serpent; so beware, be wise, and be peaceful within yourself, and beware, be wise, and be peaceful with others. Listen to the Holy Spirit and control the beast.

Angels, unborn spirits, demons, and devils all like life on earth and desire to be reborn, quickly returning to live on earth. Now that you are here on earth, alive, and living, why the hurry? Why the anger? Why the evil? Why the greed?

Give praise to the Creator God and our Lord Jesus Christ. Be happy, be peaceful with yourself, be peaceful with others, and love your neighbor as yourself.

As issued by Jesus Christ, we should work together to make life better for all. Rejoice in and enjoy all the things that God made, as well as all the things that humans have created. The beast—tamed and untamed, craving and ferocious, elusive, ugly, and fearful—is animalistic in nature. This aspect of humanity, like a leopard or tiger, can lead the human spirit to commit evil. God is the source of all living things, including the earth, which has both a physical and a divine aspect. He assigned angels various duties to assist, help, and care for all that He created, including humans, both physically and spiritually. The angels use God's energy in good ways as they transform and perform their duties.

The Antichrist, Satan, can also transform and misuse God's energy in evil ways to attack, harm, control, and kill God's children. Angels and demons fight on behalf of physical beings.

From the Bible, we learn that Adam was made from the dust of the earth and the breath of God. We are Adam and Eve—male and female, husband and wife—and we are partly human and partly divine. They were childish, primitive, pure, and innocent. The man had become as one of us, knowing good and evil. Their senses of awareness had increased to a level of maturity.

Adam and his wife heard the voice of God in the garden and were afraid, hiding themselves from the presence of the Lord God. The fear of the Lord is the beginning of knowledge. They didn't want to see each other's nakedness, nor did they want God to see their nakedness. Something had changed; their human eyes and senses had opened, and they could see and understand the differences in themselves. They were now conscious of their nakedness, sewed fig leaves, and hid themselves. Their minds, brains, human instincts, and feelings were now functioning.

Eve saw that the tree was good for food, pleasant to the eyes, and desirable to make one wise. Eve was able to discern the difference between male and female, and she showed Adam. Now they were conscious of it. The serpent knew that Adam would not pay him any attention, so he went to Eve. They knew that nakedness was bad and that covering it up was good. Humans are materialistic, physical, and spiritual in nature. We possess knowledge of good and evil; only God is perfect.

Adam and Eve had grown up; they recognized that they were male and female. Therefore, the Lord God let them go. He sent them out. Adam and Eve had learned to think like God and to think like humans. God's ways are higher than human ways. It is man's decision to do well or to do evil. God loved them and cared about them but was very angry. "What is this that thou hast done?" He told Adam and Eve about the hardships and suffering they would encounter. He forgave them, but their minds remained altered; they passed this on to their children and to all humanity from generation to generation.

The first evil was committed by Cain when he murdered his brother Abel; from then on, evil has continued. In the book of Hebrews, God said, "All shall know me." Indeed, we all know God. He is divine. The Holy Spirit of God within us gives every man and every woman their heartbeat—sons and daughters of God. Sometimes, we either obey the Holy Spirit and act in a godly manner or obey the flesh and act in a human manner. We know God; we know the devil.

The mind is restless and is everywhere. It thinks of all things, both good and evil; don't do everything it tells you. Jesus Christ prayed, "Let your will be done, not my will but yours." The will is a powerful force and can lead to great good or great evil, and those who choose to do evil with it will receive their own reward from God.

Humans are both heavenly and earthly beings. We did not come to earth on our own; God brought us here. He created the earth for us, making everything we will need available. Our knowledge, creativity, peace, love, joy, sense of awareness, and care for everything around us are reminders that God, the Creator, is our Father.

The Lord is merciful and forgiving, asking us to repent. Do not let your hearts be troubled; love God by loving one another, helping one another, seeing the good in yourself, and seeing the good in others. Be peaceful, do no harm to yourself, and do no harm to another person.

In the book of Genesis, when human beings began to increase in number on the earth and daughters were born to them, the sons of God saw that the daughters of humans were beautiful, and they married any of them they chose. Then the Lord said, "My spirit will not contend with humans forever, for they are mortal; their days will be a hundred and twenty years." The spirit of God lives forever; the flesh, the physical mortal aspect of humans, lives for a hundred and twenty years. How many people live up to 125 years today? Back then, humans lived longer; Methuselah lived for 969 years.

Humans are competing with God. He said, "My spirit will not contend with the spirit of humans forever." Perhaps if we humans stop contending with and going against God, we will live much longer.

After the flood, God promised, "Never again will all life be destroyed by the waters of a flood; never again will there be a flood to destroy living creatures on the earth." And God said, "This is the sign of the covenant I am making between Me and you and every living creature with you, a covenant for all generations to come. I have set My rainbow in the clouds, and it will be the sign of the covenant between Me and the earth. Whenever I bring clouds over the earth and the rainbow appears in the clouds, I will remember My covenant between Me and you and all living creatures of every kind. Whenever the rainbow appears in the clouds, I will see it and remember the everlasting covenant between Me and all living creatures of every kind on the earth."

How many of us pay attention to the rainbow when it appears in the sky? God mourned for Adam and Eve, Cain and Abel, and Noah's time, and He continues to mourn today. There is now more temptation, deception, and confusion. "I will never again curse the ground for man's sake, although the imaginations of man's heart are evil from his youth."

The appearance of a rainbow in the clouds is a reminder to God and a sign to humans that we are doing something wrong in His sight and that He is forgiving us. We should thank the Lord God, for He has seen our wrongdoings and has remembered an everlasting covenant between Him and all living creatures of every kind on the earth and has forgiven us.

Storms come in various forms: natural storms and human storms. Natural storms include hurricanes, tsunamis, snowstorms, earthquakes, thunder, fires, heavy rains, and overflowing rivers. The wind can be peaceful, friendly, and invisible; at other times, it is unfriendly, violent, and destructive. Nothing stands in its way. Trees and houses are thrown down, and its effects can be seen by human eyes.

Human-related storms involve sickness and illness, including stroke, heart attack, cancer, kidney failure, and lung infections, as well as war and environmental contamination. In both cases, sometimes life is lost, and sometimes life is preserved.

God the Father is the Creator. The energy from God the Father flows through God the Son, who is the Savior and the Preserver. The energy from God the Son flows through God the Holy Spirit. God the Holy Spirit exists between the divine world and the physical world, while the soul is positioned between God the Holy Spirit and the human mind. From there, the energy flows through to every member of the human body, the flesh, and the physical living being.

The soul is in contact with God the Holy Spirit and the human spirit. The body is the temple, the physical aspect—a complete housing made by God—through which we experience all things and express our feelings, compete, produce, entertain, perform, and relate to one another and the world. If the deeds of the flesh are good, God is pleased. "This is my beloved Son, in whom I am well pleased." The soul will rise toward God the Holy Spirit. If the deeds of the flesh are evil, the soul will descend from God down toward the human spirit; the soul that sins shall die.

What sin did Adam and Eve commit? Adam knew his wife, Eve, after God had sent them out of the Garden of Eden. The temptation and fall of man are detailed in the book of Genesis. The Lord God took the man and put him in the garden to tend and keep it. God said, "You have heeded the voice of your wife and have eaten of the tree of which I commanded you, saying, "You shall not eat of it."

Adam, alone with God, was good and perfect, and then God made Eve. Adam was paying close attention and listening to the voice of Eve. God placed him in the garden to tend and keep it. God is a spirit. Adam and Eve were both divine and physical; they had the mind of God and human awareness and consciousness. They talked to God and to one another.

As you know, Moses was with God in the wilderness for forty years, and he wrote the book of Genesis. Were they in love? Were they angry and quarreling? The serpent gave the fruit to Eve, and Eve gave it to Adam.

The works of the flesh are manifest: adultery, fornication, uncleanness, lasciviousness, idolatry, witchcraft, hatred, violence, emulations, wrath, strife, seditions, and heresies. But the fruit of the Spirit is love, joy, peace, longsuffering, gentleness, goodness, and faith.

Adam and Eve were exploring, doing their own will and not the will of God. The Lord God did not want Adam to be alone; He made him a helper, Eve. I can only imagine that, between them, they learned and thought to use their human senses and perceptions. The Garden of Eden is peaceful and harmonious; everything glows. Movement is effortless, with roads made of gold, and leaves that tickle the angels. Sing chorus: no harm, no threat.

The Lord's Prayer

Our Father which art in heaven,
Hallowed be thy name.
Thy kingdom come,
Thy will be done in earth,
as it is in heaven.
Give us this day our daily bread.
And forgive us our debts,
as we forgive our debtors.
And lead us not into temptation,
but deliver us from evil:
For thine is the kingdom,
and the power,
and the glory, forever.
Amen.

Doing good is the will of God above, while doing evil is the will of humans—the devil. God loves us and wants to protect us; He does not want anything evil to happen to us. Today and tomorrow, we don't know what lies ahead of us. God knows and has seen it all. Anything that is evil He will not grant to us, His children.

Live on earth, go to heaven, and avoid hell, then return to earth. In God's likeness, He created Adam and placed him in the Garden. Everything that God created looked nothing like Adam, and Adam was lonely. God caused Adam to fall deeply asleep, took one of his ribs, and made him a companion—partner and friend—Eve.

Eve cared for Adam and gave him much attention. Adam thought more of God and the care of all the things in the Garden of Eden. He saw Eve as a friend, paying no attention to her appearance. Adam was closer to God, while Eve was closer to Adam. They were both naked and aware of their differences; they were not ashamed and did not understand the purpose of those differences.

Soon, Eve understood the purposes of their differences. They were naked and glowing, walking inside the Garden of Eden in opposite directions toward each other, as if searching for something. Eve noticed Adam and stared at him. Adam, walking ahead, did not notice Eve. She walked across to him, touched him on the shoulder, and then Adam felt and noticed her.

They hugged, held each other's hands, walked down the hill, and sat under the tree.

Chapter 3

LIGHT AND DARKNESS CHRIST MIND AND CARNAL MIND

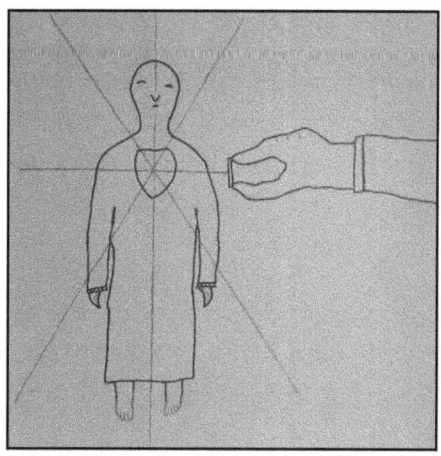

The closer you are to the light, the more you see; the farther you are from the light, the less you see. Let your light shine before men so that they may see your good works and glorify your Father in heaven. As long as you are in the world, you are the light of the world.

The light and darkness that Jesus Christ teaches us are not about the sun and the moon, nor about days and nights; they are about the Holy Spirit or God's light and man's or human light. Jesus Christ prayed, "Not my will, but let your will be done." It is about the good Samaritan and the bad Samaritan—your good deeds and bad deeds.

Being a Good Samaritan is about helping your fellow human who is in need and preserving the earth and its creatures. The Christ mind and the carnal mind—our thoughts and actions—control the light within us. We humans are more than our physical appearance; we exist in different dimensions, offering God's services to one another. Our differences are a mystery sealed by God.

A conscious mind is the awareness of yourself—who you are, your intentions, and all things around you, alive and active. Free will is the freedom God has given us—the chance to think, learn, know, experience, and make decisions about all the things around us using our senses: vision, taste, touch, hearing, speech, and smell. The subconscious mind is engaged in prayer, meditation, relaxation, dreams, and focused learning. The two minds work together.

When the conscious mind is fully active, the subconscious mind slows down; and when the subconscious mind is fully active, the conscious mind slows down. The knowledge of good and evil is the ability of humans to preserve and to destroy; we know what is right, and we know what is wrong.

The light shines in darkness, and the darkness cannot overcome it. Good is the Holy Spirit of God, eternal life; evil is the spirit of humans, death. When we do good things, it affects people—they are pleased and happy, and God is glorified. When we do evil things, it also affects people—they are not pleased, and they are not happy.

"You all know me," said Jesus Christ. Yes, indeed, we all know God. Each time you speak the truth, you know God; and each time you lie, you deny God. We are conscious of our feelings, decisions, and actions; yes, we know God. Good and evil exist; this knowledge is an efficient and helpful mechanism to not do evil but to do well and fight against evil.

Our body is the temple, the housing of God; He created us to be great, good, and wonderful. It is important to pay attention to what we bring into our bodies. A little pain in any part of our body can frighten us. Take good care of your body, and avoid things that will cause harm, pain, and sickness. God above will protect you from all danger and evil. Don't let the devil use you; don't do evil. Don't join an evil person in committing evil. All that you need, God has. Say no to the devil; he does not fulfill all your needs.

Before, sacrifices were made to wash away sin from humanity; these were temporary solutions, as sacrifices upon sacrifices were not pure enough. God loves us and has provided a permanent solution that will cleanse away sins forever, freeing the soul from death and granting us access to His presence in heaven.

Spiritually, I am bigger and larger than my physical appearance. The Holy Spirit of God lives in me. I have access to the tree of life; inseparably, I live in the temple, the heavenly mansion. In the presence of God, a pillar extends from earth to heaven, guarded by angels. God's light shines continuously in our minds and hearts.

The help we render brings out the light in us and also brings out the light in others. "My cup runs over" (Psalm 23:5). In Matthew 10:8, Jesus Christ said to the apostles, "Freely you have received; freely give." We should use our God-given talents wisely to teach, heal, produce essential things, and make life better for all.

The will of God in everything is to do unto others what you want others to do unto you, to express the love of God, and to share peace, joy, harmony, good health, and happiness with all. God is everywhere; He has no size; He has no limits; He created all things and can create anything. Both man and woman are full of light, the energy of God.

God's intention is to make life better for all—to be peaceful, joyful, loving, caring, and forgiving. In all that you do—the help you give, the words you speak, your thoughts and actions, your relationships with everything around you, your kindness, your fear and love of God, and your appreciation and value for all that He created on earth—you control the light and darkness within you.

No one is completely perfect except God. If God can have mercy and forgiveness on us and give us chances to repent, then forgiveness is a universal rule, and we humans should also forgive one another for God's sake. Bitterness, wrath, and anger are wicked and evil; put them away. Be kind, caring, and helpful to one another, as God for Christ's sake has forgiven us our sins.

It is beneficial to do things in an orderly manner, as this will reduce stress, worries, and anger. Be nice to yourself; be nice to others. We have one thing in common: we are humans on earth with one God.

In the Garden of Eden, there is neither day nor night but light—the glory of God the Father, the glory of God the Son, and the glory of God the Holy Spirit shine there continuously. The human body is a transmitter and a receiver; our prayers and meditation are transmitted to heaven through the Holy Spirit.

Messages from heaven and the spirit world come to us continually through feelings, hearing, dreams, and visions from angels, as well as through the Holy Spirit. The energy of God, the crystal river of water, flows through us continually—the light that shines in the darkness, and the darkness cannot overcome it.

Divine radiance, the light energy of God within us, is like a variable resistance; more resistance means lower light, while less resistance means higher light. It increases and decreases and is always present; darkness can never extinguish it.

The light and darkness represent our resistance to and opposition against the will of God and Christ, as well as the will of our human carnal flesh—our wants and needs. How great is the light in you, and how great is the darkness in you? We breathe in and receive, and we breathe out and transmit. The light energy of God that flows through us heats our bodies and keeps us warm. Our thoughts and feelings, whether right or wrong, are radiated, transmitted, and beamed out from our bodies.

Chapter 4

GOD BLESSED ADAM AND EVE

Adam and Eve both received the breath of life from God and became living souls. "Be fruitful and multiply and replenish the earth." Adam and Eve are our first parents, the first son and daughter of God.

Behold, children are a heritage from the Lord; the fruit of the womb is a reward. (Psalm 127:3)

They were in the presence and care of God the Father; they were clothed with the garment of God—pure, holy, innocent, young, and incorrupt. In their sight, everything glowed. They saw things in their divine nature; all the creatures in the Garden of Eden obeyed Adam and Eve, and they must have noticed Eve's arrival in the garden. Together, they lived in peace and harmony—no harm and no threat—until their disobedience.

Moses was with God in the wilderness; he built the pyramids of Egypt and wrote the book of Genesis. Good and evil exist in every creature on earth. We are God's children, and He gave us dominion over the other creatures and placed them in our care.

And when the woman saw that the tree was good for food, and that it was pleasant to the eyes, Eve was enticed by the serpent. The human spirit and flesh clouded her vision; she no longer saw Adam as a friend—she desired what he had and seduced him. Together, Eve and Adam ate the forbidden fruit; they loved each other.

Then the spirit of the serpent entered them both, opened their minds and their eyes, and they saw their own nakedness. God the Father sent them out of the Garden of Eden. This all took place in the spiritual world, in the Garden of Eden.

The children of God are beautiful and attractive; you are the apple of God's eye. Some people believe that the fruit they ate was an apple, while others think it symbolizes something deeper. Indeed, God created many fruits in the forest that we do not know of. I am not certain what fruit it was, but the human figure can be referred to as an apple.

They gave birth to Cain and Abel.

That serpent, the old one called the devil, Satan, who deceives the whole world. (Revelation 12:9)

He who is in you is greater than he who is in the world. The Holy Spirit of God, the Creator, is in you; He is whom you should worship and is greater than the human beast on earth. They separated from God and left His divine heavenly presence and glory. The energy of God in them dropped to a human level. The veil was removed from their eyes, and they became aware of themselves. Now they saw things in their physical nature. They began to think as humans with body, mind, and soul. They were one with God before the temptation. Jesus said, "I and my Father are one."

Aware of themselves and the things around them, both physically and spiritually, they fell from heaven to earth, the physical world, to live and care for the earth and all that God created. Earth Day and Mother's Day should be observed as worldwide public holidays.

Were they immortal? How long did they stay with God the Father before He sent them out of the Garden of Eden to live on their own on a big and lonely planet, Earth—frightened and terrified? What language did they speak? What did they eat? How did they survive the weather and wild beasts? How did they meet their needs? Did God send an angel to help them?

What exactly is this forbidden fruit that led to the separation of man from his Creator? What happened between Adam and Eve? What did they do that altered their minds? As humans, only the two of them were in the garden, but the serpent gave the fruit to them. Who was the serpent? Did Adam charm Eve? Did Eve seduce Adam? The serpent represents the human spirit, flesh, and blood—earthly. Good and evil are combined in the human mind.

There are two kinds of nakedness: physical nakedness, which is the natural exposure of the body, and spiritual nakedness, which is the removal of the garment of God due to feelings and pleasure. Knowledge is gained by looking, learning, observing, hearing, and thinking. Obviously, this involves the eyes and the mind.

The fig tree is mentioned several times in the Bible:

"Early in the morning, as Jesus was on his way back to the city, he was hungry. Seeing a fig tree by the road, he went up to it but found nothing on it except leaves. Then he said to it, "May you never bear fruit again." (Matthew 21:19)

Fig seeds can be carried around by birds and animals. The seeds can grow in many places: on roofs, on trees, and in the soil. The fig tree's roots spread and twist around the stem of the tree it grows on, from the stem down to the ground. The fig tree's branches and leaves grow and spread above, suppressing the tree it grows on. And so are our sins. (Mark 8:24)

They brought a blind man to Jesus Christ; He spit on his eyes, placed His hands upon him, and asked him what he saw. He looked up and said, "I see men walking like trees." In the spiritual dimension, we are like trees. God planted us to bear good fruit and do good things.

Unlike the fig tree, physically, humans are conscious of their intentions. We know when we are right and when we are wrong; we know good and evil. Our sins grow, causing stress and sickness, polluting and draining the pure river of water. The Holy Spirit is in control when we do well and bear good fruit; the pure river of water will flow through us abundantly.

God is truth and light; He owns everything in heaven and on earth and lacks nothing. We desire both heavenly and earthly things, which represent our wants and needs—human desire.

Angel or devil, heaven or hell—the choice is yours; the soul is the benefactor. Jesus came into this world so that humanity could live a better life.

All judgment, power, and authority have been given to the Son, Jesus Christ, the Lamb of God, full of mercy and forgiveness. He has assigned angels various duties to assist humans. He judges who goes to heaven, who goes to hell, and who returns to earth. He forgives sins, but not all sins. Heaven is not full, and hell is not empty. Souls go through purification, restoration, and rebirth.

There was no temptation of man until Eve's arrival. We are partly divine and partly human. Adam and Eve ate the forbidden fruit, and as it is said, "the love of money is the root of all evil." Back then, there was no money, but now there is.

Adam only knew his wife after God the Father sent them out of the Garden of Eden. The spirit of God and the spirit of man live in one body. It is not what goes into a human that defiles him or her, but the words that come out of their mouth, along with their thoughts, feelings, and actions. Adam and Eve lived with God; they talked to God. The serpent gave the fruit to Eve—desirable and good for food. Adam was attracted to Eve, and he charmed her. Eve liked Adam, and there were feelings and communication between them. Adam gave Eve what she needed, and Eve gave Adam what he needed. They activated, gravitated, magnetized, energized, and ignited one another.

Nothing else mattered—just the two of them. They belonged together, and the world belonged to them. Welcome to the physical world.

God is the source of all knowledge. All knowledge is useful, depending on how you use it and what you do with it—whether to help or harm someone. There are very powerful and magical leaves, grass, herbs, and fruits in the forest that we do not yet know of. Adam had never seen another physical human before, and neither had Eve. Their strange and sudden appearance must have been a frightening and shocking moment for them, and God was present for the introduction and presentation.

They noticed the differences in themselves, turned on each other, and became afraid, so they went into hiding and sewed fig leaves to cover themselves. Adam and Eve both saw the fruit, but Eve had a greater desire to eat it.

The things created and made by God are uncountable, glorious, and priceless—precious, beautiful, sweet, charming, enticing, and hard to resist.

They now possessed the power of light and the power of darkness. Angels are messengers of God, sent to save and protect humanity. The devil is the messenger of Satan, deceiving and confusing humans. Angels are higher beings; the devil is a lower being.

Let us do things God's way. Praise the Lord, for He has overcome evil and death for us. Today, there are many Adams and Eves to be tempted. The temptation continues, the disobedience continues, the rebellion continues, and the forbidden fruit remains forbidden.

God placed us here to tend to the Garden of Eden, which is the earth. We work for God through peace, love, and compassion. He distributes resources and assistance to all. Love your neighbor as yourself.

Fighting or killing your fellow human is evil knowledge and wrong in the eyes of humanity and God. Wars and weapons of mass destruction are knowledge of evil, a threat to humanity, a threat to nature, and a threat to every living thing that God created. They will cause massive death, massive destruction, and massive contamination, affecting our destiny.

God the Father is the Creator and has power over everything. He will protect the earth and all its inhabitants from these weapons. Do you remember the flood during Noah's time? He has other ways; God is above and watching us. For now, He allows things to play out. Man did not create the earth; he may rule it, but he does not control it. The Antichrist, who seeks to harm and destroy God's work, will be destroyed. God will rule the earth and lead us with peace, love, joy, happiness, good health, and harmony.

We humans are born as babies, and as we grow, so do our abilities to feel, think, know, understand, and make our own decisions. We compete, entertain, crack jokes, and win or lose. God loves us; we are emotional beings, easy to please and easy to offend. Little things make us happy, peaceful, joyful, nice, loving, and kind. Yet little things can also make us angry, mad, sad, mean, evil, and hateful.

We are guarded by God's laws, the laws of nature, and human laws—through both obedience and disobedience. There are moments in our lifetime when we feel as though we are in the Garden of Eden, in the presence of God, like children. Everything glows with divine harmony—charming, friendly, peaceful, and harmless. Yet it becomes harmful in the absence of God. We touch everything and play with everything. Like children, we want every candy, every toy, regardless of the cost.

From the beginning, God did not send His children, Adam and Eve, to the physical earth; He kept them. Dinosaurs and other creatures lived on earth, perhaps as part of an experiment. They failed, lacking the ability to improve and make use of the earth's natural resources.

Paradise Earth is the most beautiful planet in the universe; there is more than enough of everything for us humans, over and over again.

God created everything so that we can all rejoice, be pleased, and be happy wherever we are. Humans are satisfied with who they are and what they have; they do not want to run out of what they possess.

As life evolves, humanity advances, continuously working, producing, and replacing old devices. See the beautiful and wonderful things God the Father has made; He has blessed us with greater things. Indeed, the quality of life and advancements in technology are on the rise. We have conquered, improved, multiplied, and now we want more—like the Tower of Babel and today's skyscrapers.

God is greater than man; the things God has made are many. He has given us more than we could ever consume. If we could consume them, we would be satisfied, but we can never fully do so. The closer we are to God, the greater and better our lives will become.

All that the Father has is mine. He will take of mine and give to us the power, wisdom, and knowledge of God, which comes from above, through Christ, to us.

Chapter 5

THE TREE OF LIFE RETURN OF THE PRODIGAL SON

Likewise, I say unto you, there is joy in the presence of the angels of God over one sinner that repents. (Luke 15:10)

God sent His only Son into the world to free us from the sins of Adam; in Jesus Christ, we are free and alive. When a sinner on earth repents and returns to God, the angels in heaven rejoice and celebrate for the newborn in heaven.

He placed at the east of the Garden of Eden cherubim and a flaming sword, which turned every way to guard the tree of life. First, Adam received the breath of life and became a living being. The tree of knowledge of good and evil is mortal; it does not live forever. The second Adam, Jesus Christ, is a life-giving spirit; the tree of life lives forever, immortal. The tree of life is between the Divine world and the Physical world.

The beginning of life was in the Garden of Eden. Paradise on earth—heaven—is a spiritual, divine place, and in it, God created everything. God the Father is the Creator; the Son is the Preserver; the Holy Spirit is the Spirit of God within you. The soul and the human spirit are the destroyers. The Holy Spirit of God, the soul, and the flesh make up the entire human body, the physical being. The soul is between the Holy Spirit and the human spirit—the living being. The divine self is your godly aspect, and the physical is the human aspect; together, they function.

The pure river of the water of life is as clear as crystal, flowing from the throne of God and the throne of the Lamb, to the throne of grace. In the midst of the street, between the divine and the physical, was the tree of life—the Holy Spirit. There shall be no more curses; the throne of the Lamb shall be in it.

"I will arise and go to my father, and will say unto him, "Father, I have sinned against heaven and before thee, and I am no more worthy to be called thy son." And he arose and came to his father. But when he was yet a great way off, his father saw him and had compassion, and ran, and fell on his neck, and kissed him. And the son said unto him, "Father, I have sinned against heaven and in thy sight, and I am no more worthy to be called thy son."

But the father said to his servants, "Bring forth the best robe, and put it on him; and put a ring on his hand, and shoes on his feet. And bring hither the fatted calf, and kill it, and let us eat and be merry. For this my son was dead, and is alive again; he was lost, and is found." And they began to be merry.

Now his elder son was in the field, and as he came and drew nigh to the house, he heard music and dancing. And he called one of the servants and asked what these things meant. And he said unto him, "Thy brother is come, and thy father hath killed the fatted calf because he hath received him safe and sound." And he was angry and would not go in. Therefore, his father came out and entreated him.

And he, answering, said to his father, "Lo, these many years do I serve thee, neither transgressed I at any time thy commandment: and yet thou never gavest me a kid, that I might make merry with my friends. But as soon as this thy son has come, who has devoured thy living with harlots, thou hast killed for him the fatted calf."

And he said unto him, "Son, thou art ever with me, and all that I have is thine. It was meet that we should make merry and be glad: for this thy brother was dead and is alive again; and was lost and is found." (Luke 15:18–32)

"See that you do not despise these little ones, for I tell you that in Heaven their angels always see the face of my Father." (Matthew 18:10)

When you are around two-year-olds or four-year-olds having their birthday party, you see that they glow. They are beautiful, loving, and full of wonder; and that is how God the Father sees our angels when we come and behold His face in Heaven.

The soul is the immortal animating principle of the living human. Human nature—the flesh—whether doing well or doing wrong, needs the soul to function. Jesus Christ prayed, "Not my will, but Your will be done." It's about God's will versus human will. God is spirit, and the Holy Spirit of God is with the human soul.

O wretched man that I am! Who shall deliver me from the body of this death? I thank God through Jesus Christ our Lord.

So then, with the mind I serve the law of God, but with the flesh, the law of sin. (Romans 7:14-25)

"Command that these stones be made bread; if thou be the Son of God, cast thyself down; all these things will I give thee if thou wilt fall down and worship me." (Matthew 4:3)

Jesus Christ fasted for forty days and forty nights. He was in God's Spirit, and He was hungry. The devil, the tempter, said, "Use God's power. Turn these stones to bread and satisfy the flesh. Reduce God's energy down to a human level."

The return of the prodigal son is not an easy task, for the human soul is weighed down by the wants and needs of the human flesh. God the Son, Jesus Christ, said, "No one comes to the Father except by me"—the tree of life, the Holy Spirit.

That is what the soul must climb to arise and return to the Father. This brother was dead and is alive again; he was lost and is found. "I will arise and go to my father." This task is not a physical journey; it is a divine spiritual journey that manifests in different ways through several realms—from the physical world to the divine world, from earth to heaven, from the mortal world to the immortal world. From the finite world, earth, to the infinite world, heaven—this is the return of the prodigal son to God the Father.

This is not an easy task, for the human soul is weighed down by the wants and emotional needs of the flesh. Can you pass?

All the temptations that you face—what is impossible for humans is possible for God. Seek it genuinely through prayer, fasting, meditation, going to church, reading the Bible, and obeying the golden rule issued by Jesus Christ: "Do unto others what you would want others to do unto you." And there shall be no more curses because the throne of the Lamb shall be in it. You don't have to endure these temptations and crucifixion. Jesus Christ has gone through them for you and paid the price of death on the cross for our sins, for you and me.

To start, read the Bible—the book of John. Keep it by your bedside. At bedtime, read, pay attention, and understand the words. Pray to God and call on Jesus Christ.

"Seek, and you will find. Ask, and you will be given. Knock, and the door will open."

God, we come to You in response to Your call. Your soul will cry out to the Holy Spirit. The Holy Spirit will call on the Son, Jesus Christ; and the Son will call on God the Father. God will hear your prayer and respond to your call and needs. His energy, the Holy Ghost, from above will come down to your need during the baptism of the soul.

If the Spirit of God that raised Jesus from the dead dwells in you, it will quicken your mortal body and keep it alive. The energy of God, the Holy Spirit, will activate your Christ mind and deactivate your carnal mind. Your soul will rise up to the Holy Spirit, and you will begin the journey from earth to the tree of life in the Garden of Eden.

You land at the tree of life, holding onto the branch of the tree of life safely. It controls and stabilizes your landing. You swing up and down, holding onto the branch of the tree of life. You have landed in the Garden of Eden and are frightened by the presence of two lions—one on the right and one on the left—who chase you.

Leap by leap, hop by hop, you ascend higher and higher, out of the reach of the lions. You ascend further into heaven to the throne of grace, the throne of the Lamb, and return to God the Father.

The Garden of Eden can also be viewed as the third heaven. From Genesis 2:9 to 3:8–24, Adam represents the tree of the knowledge of good and evil. God the Father is the tree of life. Adam and Eve were sent out of the Garden of Eden due to disobedience. They heard the voice of the Lord God in the Garden of Eden.

At times, God the Father from above does speak to us, and sometimes we hear the voice of God and feel His presence and movement. The Lord God sent them out from the Garden of Eden down to earth to till the ground from which they were taken and placed at the east gate of the Garden of Eden, cherubim to keep the way to the tree of life.

Access to the tree of life in the Garden of Eden and to God the Father is made possible by our Lord Jesus Christ; He has opened the way. Every living being is already on the path.

"I am the way, the truth, and the life; no man cometh unto the Father but by me." (John 14:6)

Jesus is the Alpha and the Omega, the beginning and the end of creation, the breath of life, the second Adam, the Son, and the life-giving Spirit. Through Him, God created all things. Today, we can all, through Jesus Christ, eat of the tree of life and find our way to God the Father.

Jesus was tempted three times: He turned stones into bread. "Man shall not live by bread alone." "If you are the Son of God, throw yourself down. You shall not tempt the Lord your God." "All these things I will give you if you will fall down and worship me." You shall worship the Lord your God, and Him alone you shall serve.

Adam and Eve were tempted. They obeyed and worshiped the serpent. They ate the forbidden fruit, fell from grace, failed all temptations, and were sent out of the Garden of Eden into the physical world. What could have happened if Adam and Eve had resisted temptation? God the Father would have been pleased: "This is my beloved Son, in whom I am well pleased."

Without sin, there would be no curse, no separation from God, no suffering, and no sickness to access the tree of life. We should have the mind of Christ, filled with more peace, love, joy, and harmony, and less evil. Don't murder. Live longer, without war and fighting, but with more intelligence, greater advancement, and so on.

Humans are insatiable. Well, how can we be satisfied? We are greedy, and most of our thoughts and quests revolve around material things. How can you be satisfied when what is inside you is greater than what is outside you? God knows that nothing will truly satisfy man. The wants and needs of the flesh are very consuming, and in some cases, they drag the temple's energy and that of the soul to a low level.

Everything you do on earth is recorded in heaven—dangerous and careless lifestyles and improper use of God-given energy and talents. Well, God is kind, righteous, loving, and forgiving. The earth will not be empty; it will be filled with His mercy and forgiveness. We are continuously forgiven and renewed.

For human satisfaction, we need to seek the Holy Spirit of God. We must make every effort to rejoice and be thankful to God for ourselves and for others. To be satisfied, we must realize and know that God is our Father; He loves us and lives in us. Everything that humans create comes from studying the things that were made by God. He leads us, and we follow.

Why Are We Not Satisfied?

Some people don't want God to lead them; they do things their own way, going against God, doing evil, committing crimes, and defiling their bodies, the temple of God. Two of the trees in the Garden of Eden are the tree of the knowledge of good and evil and the tree of life; both trees bear fruit.

Well, God created heaven and earth, and we can also refer to them as the trees of heaven and the trees of earth. When Adam and Eve were sent away from the Garden of Eden, God did not separate from them completely. The Holy Spirit of God, through the soul, remained with them.

Through Adam and Eve, sin came into the world; and through Jesus Christ, sin is taken away from the world. God gave us everything freely. I can do nothing on my own; the Father does the work. God gave us different talents, and we are able to do the things that we do because He has blessed us. "Greater things shall you do;" He is with us and leading the way.

Chapter 6

THE POWER OF THE CROSS

God is a Spirit. He created the physical world and the spiritual world; He made man and woman in His own image. God knows who we are, both physically and spiritually; He understands what we are going through. He can save us and heal us, both physically and spiritually.

But if the Spirit of Him who raised up Jesus from the dead dwells in you, He who raised up Christ from the dead shall also quicken your mortal bodies by His Spirit that dwells in you. (Romans 8:11)

O death, where is thy sting? O grave, where is thy victory? The sting of death is sin, and the strength of sin is the law. Thanks be to God, who gives us the victory through our Lord Jesus Christ.

He rose, and the grave was empty. He lived, and the grave was defeated. He appeared, talked, and dined with the apostles. He is alive. He descended to the lowest; He is the Alpha. He ascended into the highest heaven; He is the Omega, King of Kings. God has delivered me from going down to the pit, and I shall live to enjoy the light of life.

God does all these things for a person twice, even thrice: forgive, save, and turn them back from the pit of death so that the light of life may shine on them. Jesus Christ, dying on the cross, pleaded, "Forgive them, Father, for they know not what they are doing."

Jesus Christ was put to death, nailed and bound to the cross. He died on the cross, descended with the cross, and God the Father raised Him up with the cross. He ascended into heaven with the cross. He delivered me from going down to the lowest; He balanced the scale for me. Raised up from the lowest, I ascend upward toward the middle. I ascend to the middle; I and my Father are one. I feel the divine radiance; the separation is removed.

As a human, you do not need to die in order to experience these things. Jesus Christ has died for you. He will guard you, lead you, show you, and take you safely across to and from.

Let this mind be in you, which is also in Christ Jesus—the Christ mind, instead of the carnal mind. The scale of life records and measures all your deeds: the things you did right and the things you did wrong.

I sit at the left hand of God the Father Almighty, which is the left side of the judgment scale. Your Savior, Jesus Christ, the Lamb of God who takes away the sins of the world, sits at the right hand of God the Father Almighty.

First, the weight of my good deeds is placed on the right side of the scale; then the weight of my wrong deeds is placed on the left. All have sinned and come short of the glory of God.

You rise above when your good deeds are enough to balance the scale, and you descend when your wrong deeds are greater. Then the Lamb of God, who takes away the sins of the world, is placed on the right side; He balances the judgment scale for me, and I rise up from the pit of death.

You cannot be as spotless as the Lamb; you must do many good things to please God and balance the scale on your own. All you need to do now is accept Jesus Christ as your Savior and allow Him to lead and be in control of your life.

Let the dead bury the dead. The first death is physical, human, natural death, and the second death is spiritual death—separation from God. This occurs when Christ's mind is not in control, and the carnal mind takes over.

In either case, it is a continuous learning process. The soul lives; it goes through purification, rebirth, and back to physical life—a chance for you to learn, accept Christ, and repent from evil and wrongdoing.

You either allow the Holy Spirit of God to control you or the flesh to control you—Christ's mind or the carnal mind.

If the Spirit of God leads you, then you are alive, even though your mortal body is dead, separated from God due to sin. The Spirit of God will keep you alive. Having Christ in you does not make you sinless. The Christ mind is a mediator, a link between you and God. It allows you to gradually grow and do things God's way—a better life for you and others.

God gave Adam and Eve both the Christ mind and the carnal mind. In the beginning, Adam and Eve had no sin, and only the Christ mind was active in them. They were in the presence of God and talked to Him always. Adam and Eve activated the carnal mind when they ate the forbidden fruit. The divine radiance of God in them diminished and was debased to a human level—more humanity and less divinity—aware and conscious of their physical flesh. They attracted one another, corrupted in the sight of God, and they passed it on to us.

For God so loved the world, He gave His beloved Son; He incarnated and came into the world. Those who are led by the flesh cannot please God. Except a man be born of water and of the Spirit, he cannot enter into the kingdom of God. That which is born of the flesh is flesh, and that which is born of the Spirit is spirit.

The wind blows where it wishes, and you hear the sound of it but cannot tell whence it comes and whither it goes; so is everyone who is born of the Spirit. For to be carnally minded is death, but to be spiritually minded is life and peace. Because the carnal mind is enmity against God; for it is not subject to the law of God, nor indeed can it be.

So then, those who are in the flesh cannot please God; but you are not in the flesh, but in the Spirit, the Holy Spirit. And if Christ is in you, then the Spirit of God dwells in you.

Yet a little while, and the world will see Me no more; but you see Me: because I live, you shall live also. For as many as are led by the Spirit of God, they are the sons of God.

This is cause and effect, action and reaction. One's deeds have a corresponding effect. The Holy Spirit of God is incorruptible and lives in us, washing away our sins and renewing us continuously. Do not judge, or you too will be judged; in the same way you judge others, you will be judged; and with the measure you use, it will be measured to you. How can you say to your brother, "Let me take the speck out of your eye," when all the time there is a beam in your own eye? First, take the beam out of your own eye, and then you will see clearly to remove the speck from your brother's eye.

We don't know each other's thoughts; only God knows my thoughts, and only God knows your thoughts. He alone can judge us correctly. Forming opinions about others without knowing all about them can lead you to incorrect judgments and decisions. Cool down and control your anger; control the beast. Peace brings love and goodness, forgiveness, and healing. Control your anger and avoid confrontation.

We are humans with sins and errors. Let your cup of joy run over; wish one another peace, love, and joy. Allow the crystal river of water from above to flow through you completely; think like Christ; see the work of God and the wonderful godly nature in us humans. Blessed are the peacemakers, for they shall see God. Do not give dogs what is sacred; do not throw your pearls to pigs. If you do, they may trample them under their feet and turn and tear you to pieces.

God, the Creator of heaven and earth, is our Father and dwells within us. He built the earth for us and placed everything we need upon it.

The golden rule in everything is to do to others what you would have them do to you. How great is the darkness in you, and how great is the light in you, is the result of how you use the free will God gave you—for good or for evil. You should know that in everything we do, God sees us all. Sons and daughters, brothers and sisters, keep your body, mind, and soul balanced. Enjoy the earth, enjoy heaven, avoid hell, do no harm to yourself, and do no harm to others.

May the mercy of God, good health, prosperity, longevity, peace, love, and joy be upon you; let your soul delight itself in abundance and pleasure. Nothing is hidden from the sight of the Lord. From His heavenly throne above, He sees us all in great multitudes, going in different directions and doing different things.

In the book of Mark, He was transfigured, and Elijah and Moses appeared. In the book of Matthew, Christ Jesus walked on the sea.

Immediately, Jesus made His disciples get into the boat and go before Him to the other side. He went up on the mountain by Himself to pray. Now, in the fourth watch of the night, Jesus went to them, walking on the sea. When the disciples saw Him walking on the sea, they were troubled, saying, "It is a ghost." But immediately, Jesus spoke to them, saying, "Be of good cheer; it is I. Do not be afraid."

And Peter answered Him, saying, "Lord, if it is You, command me to come to You on the water." So He said, "Come." And when Peter had come down out of the boat, he walked on the water to go to Jesus.

But when he saw that the wind was boisterous, he was afraid; and beginning to sink, he cried out, saying, "Lord, save me!" And immediately, Jesus stretched out His hand and caught him.

God, incarnate in human form, blessed us with greater things. If you can do some of the things He did, we say you can equate yourself with Jesus Christ. However, if you indeed equate yourself with Jesus Christ, you will certainly need His support, the support of ascended masters, and the support of angels to do the things He did. Even if one is able to perform the same miracles that Jesus Christ did while He was on earth in human form, that does not make that person equal to Jesus Christ.

Equating oneself with Jesus Christ is good, inspiring, helpful, and encouraging. In this age of technological advancement, mass media, weapons of mass destruction, and population growth, it is highly needed; we require prophets and messengers to visit and spend time with us.

As children, we often sin. We must admit that we have sinned and, like children, come to God to ask for forgiveness.

In Mark 10:35-40, Zebedee's sons, James and John, came to Jesus Christ, asking, "Grant that in heaven we may sit on your right and on your left." Jesus asked them, "Are you able to drink the cup that I drink, or be baptized with the baptism I am baptized with?" They replied, "Yes." He said to them, "You shall drink from the cup that I drink from and be baptized with the baptism I am baptized with; but to sit on my right and on my left is not mine to give."

"Father, all things are possible unto Thee; take away this cup from me: nevertheless, not what I will, but what you will be done." The cups symbolize His suffering and death on the cross for our freedom and deliverance—a good life. Jesus Christ had no sins; He suffered, was arrested, went through judgments, was crucified, and resurrected.

When He said, "Take this cup from me," He was referring to the suffering and death on the cross for our sins. Like Jesus Christ, we humans go through suffering, death, judgment, and resurrection. Like the Zebedee brothers, we can drink from the cup and be baptized with the baptism. Where we sit and where we go is decided in heaven by God the Father and His angels.

Regarding the baptism of the human flesh: "I indeed baptize you unto repentance, but he who is coming after me is mightier than I, whose sandals I am not worthy to carry." (Matthew 3:11)

Peter was the head of the disciples and had been with Jesus Christ. He walked on water to go to Jesus, but when he took his eyes away from Him, saw the wind, and was afraid, he began to sink. They were troubled, saying, "It is a ghost." No, it is not a ghost. Just as Jesus Christ was transfigured, Elijah and Moses appeared. It is Jesus Christ, God the Son, walking on the sea.

He went up on the mountain by Himself to pray. He is the light of the world. He was crowned with thorns, and blood dripped from His head, face, and neck to the ground. Jesus Christ went through all these sufferings in order to remove our sin, protect us from the evil one, lead us to a better life, and bring us closer to God the Father.

Chapter 7

THE MAKER'S EYE

If the deeds of the flesh are good, God is pleased. "This is my beloved Son, in whom I am well pleased." The soul will ascend. If the deeds of the flesh are evil, the soul will descend. The soul is the inner man, the divine, the immortal aspect of man. The flesh is the outer man, the physical, earthly, mortal aspect of man. The Holy Spirit, the soul, and the flesh all function together; and through the body, they feel and experience the physical world and enjoy all the things God created.

And the Lord said, "My spirit shall not strive with man forever, for he is indeed flesh; for his days shall be one hundred and twenty years." (Genesis 6:3)

So man is a combination of both the soil of the earth and the breath of God. "My spirit shall not strive with man and shall not compete or put up with the sinful nature of man forever, for he is indeed flesh." The spirit is of God, while the flesh is from the soil of the earth. The physical world is the natural world where we live and experience all things around us. The spiritual world is the unseen world where our thoughts and feelings move around. In the divine world, heaven, the firmament, there is the throne of God and the throne of the Lamb. The spirit of God seeks truth and light; the soul is immortal, the perfect image of God.

The human flesh is mortal, outward, the imperfect image of God. Man is a mixture of everything on earth—the soil—and everything in heaven—the breath. The flesh is weak. The flesh, in its needs and desires for worldly things, requires the support of the soul to function, thereby subjecting the soul to corruption. The life you live in the physical world—obedience or disobedience—determines the separation between light and darkness and your distance from God. He created the earth pure and clean; we corrupt it by our evil thoughts, greed, crime, and anger. God is kind, patient, loving, and forgiving. We are the apple of His eye—smart or foolish, rich or poor, tall or short, black or white—He loves us.

There are different languages, different cultures, different traditions, and different religions; He loves us all equally. You build your house to live in; likewise, our body is the house of God, His temple. He made it, and He dwells in it.

"What is a man that you are mindful of him, and the son of man that you visit him? For you have made him a little lower than the angels, and you have crowned him with glory and honor. You made him to have dominion over the works of your hand; you have put all things under his feet— all sheep and oxen, even the beasts of the field, the birds of the air, and the fish of the sea, and whatsoever passes through the paths of the seas." (Psalm 8:4–8)

Many people still doubt if God, the Creator, has visited us in human form. Yes, He has visited us many times. In the book of Hebrews, the priest offered up sacrifices first for his own sin and then for the sin of the people. No sacrifice was pure enough to cleanse away the sins of the people forever. Jesus did this once and for all when He offered up Himself.

The priests themselves are not God; they are human. They offer sacrifices to wash away their own sins and then the sins of other people; these offerings are temporary. They could not wash away sins from man completely. God, our Creator, came into the world as man and offered up Himself once and for all for the forgiveness of sins. We do not judge God; He does things for our improvement and safety. He made us all. He came into the world through any tribe, anywhere He pleased, and through the Israelites.

In the book of John, it is stated, "He that hath seen me hath seen the Father. I am in the Father, and the Father is in me." Like Father, like Son.

The Father

Today, humans have advanced greatly in science and technology, and in many ways, we have pleased God by making life better and safer for all. We have built and made many things: cars, ships, planes, rockets, skyscrapers, electronic healthcare, agriculture, machinery, manufacturing, transportation, communication, education, churches, religion, entertainment, tap water, houses, toilets, and so on. We have been to the moon. Imagine what we are going to build tomorrow and where we will go tomorrow.

In many ways, we have displeased God: wars, crime, greed, corruption, weapons of mass destruction, the killing of wildlife, contamination, pollution, and so on.

The kingdom of heaven is at hand. Jesus Christ has brought it. We have it. It has come to us, and through the baptism of the soul, He links us to our God and heaven. The past era of Adam and Eve and Cain and Abel is over. This is the new heaven, the new world era of Jesus Christ.

Jesus Christ has granted us authority over all the power of the enemy; He granted us access to the tree of life. "I am in the Father, and you in Me, and I in you." All authority in heaven and on earth God gave Him, and through Christ, we partake; we benefit from all the things that God created. Greater things shall you do: heal the sick and raise the dead. Ascend to heaven.

The pure river of the water of life is clear as crystal, flowing out of the throne of God and of the Lamb, to the throne of grace. In the midst of the street, between your divine self and your physical self, was the tree of life; and there shall be no more curse because the throne of the Lamb shall be in it.

The LORD God said, "The man has now become like one of us, knowing good and evil." (Genesis 3:22)

This is the bread which cometh down from heaven, that a man may eat thereof and not die.

I am the living bread which came down from heaven: if any man eats of this bread, he shall live forever; and the bread that I will give is my flesh, which I will give for the life of the world. Verily, verily, I say unto you, except ye eat the flesh of the Son of Man and drink His blood, ye have no life in you. Whoso eats my flesh and drinketh my blood hath eternal life, and I will raise him up at the last day. For my flesh is meat indeed, and my blood is drink indeed. He that eateth my flesh and drinketh my blood dwelleth in me, and I in him. As the living Father hath sent me, and I live by the Father, so he that eateth me, even he shall live by me. This is that bread which came down from heaven: not as your fathers did eat manna and are dead; he that eateth of this bread shall live forever.

Doth this offend you? What if ye shall see the Son of Man ascend up where He was before? It is the Spirit that quickeneth; the flesh profiteth nothing: the words that I speak unto you, they are spirit, and they are life.

Then I saw a new heaven and a new earth, for the first heaven and the first earth had passed away, and there was no longer any sea. I saw the Holy City, the New Jerusalem, coming down out of heaven from God, prepared as a bride beautifully dressed for her husband. And I heard a loud voice from the throne saying, "Look! God's dwelling place is now among the people, and He will dwell with them. They will be His people, and God Himself will be with them and be their God. He will wipe every tear from their eyes. There will be no more death or mourning or crying or pain, for the old order of things has passed away."

He who was seated on the throne said, "I am making everything new." Then he said, "Write this down, for these words are trustworthy and true." He said to me, "It is done. I am the Alpha and the Omega, the Beginning and the End. To the thirsty, I will give water without cost from the spring of the water of life. Those who are victorious will inherit all this, and I will be their God, and they will be my children. But the cowardly, the unbelieving, the vile, the murderers, the sexually immoral, those who practice magic arts, the idolaters, and all liars—they will be consigned to the fiery lake of burning sulfur.

The kingdom of heaven is at hand. God's dwelling place is now among the people. The bread is the Word of God that you hear being preached in church. The flesh, blood, and wine are the life, death, and Holy Spirit of Jesus Christ that have been released on the new earth. With Adam and Eve sent out of the Garden of Eden, God the Father and God the Son remained there.

"Son, you are always with me. Your brother was lost, and now he has returned home. Eating from the tree of life does not make you God, the Creator of heaven and earth, but you become as one of them. Jesus Christ will crown you, make you king, make you lord, and make you prince—make you god—to get to the throne of God, the holiest of all."

I indeed baptize you with water unto repentance to receive Jesus Christ; Jesus Christ will baptize you with the Holy Spirit and fire unto your God. (Matthew 3:11)

Verily I say unto you, whosoever shall not receive the kingdom of God as a little child shall in no wise enter therein. (Luke 18:17)

Can you enter heaven, the kingdom of God? Well, you have to humble yourself and be spotless and sinless like the Lamb, fulfilling and sacrificing all worldly things. Adam and Eve were driven out of heaven because they failed the temptation. Can you pass it on your own? The spirit is willing, but the flesh is weak. Jesus Christ humbled Himself and endured all temptation.

These worldly things—the material world—are our desires, the tantalizing wants and needs of fleshly pleasure. You seek them from the throne of grace through Jesus Christ, my Lord, through the baptism of the soul with the Holy Ghost and fire. Jesus Christ teaches us to love our neighbor as we love ourselves and to help one another, and He revealed God the Father to us.

I proceeded forth and came from God. (John 8:42)

You have both seen Him, and it is He who is talking with you. (John 9:37)

The words that I speak to you, I do not speak on my own authority, and the word which you hear is not mine but the Father's who sent me. (John 14:10)

The Word was made flesh. Everything has a name. Without a name, it means nothing and cannot be identified nor remembered. Jesus Christ lives, and you live; his words are alive in you. Heaven and earth shall pass away, but his words shall not pass away. God incarnate came into the world and lived among us in the human (or "in human form as") Jesus Christ. He healed the sick, raised the dead, and taught us heavenly things and how to love our neighbor as ourselves.

Destroy this temple, and in three days I will raise it up.

(John 2:19)

God is above in heaven. We are humans and live (or "are") on earth. There is more work going on and taking place in heaven concerning lives and creation. Stay with God, do your part, follow the will of God, and he will take care of all your needs.

He sent prophets and angels to us. God is a spirit, and those who worship him must worship in spirit and truth.

Most assuredly, I say to you, he who believes in Me, the works that I do he will do also, and greater works than these he will do because I go to my Father; and the word which you hear is not mine but the Father's who sent me. A little while longer, and the world will see Me no more, but you will see Me because I live, and you will live also. At that day, you will know that I am in the Father and you in Me and I in you.

(John 14:12, 19–20)

In Jesus's resurrection, he appeared to the disciples, talked to them, ate with them, and vanished from their sight several times. Here, we have seen God the Son talking and eating with humans.

For what man knows the things of a man except the spirit of the man which is in him? Even so, no one knows the things of God except the Spirit of God.

(1 Corinthians 2:11)

You don't know what I am thinking, and I don't know what you are thinking, but God knows what both of us are thinking. We grow suspicious of others easily; we interpret situations based on our assumptions, only to later find out we were wrong. No one is perfect. That is how God made us; that is how we function. Try doing things God's way.

And the Lord whom you seek will suddenly come to his temple.

(Malachi 3:1)

I indeed baptize you with water unto repentance to receive Jesus Christ; Jesus Christ will baptize you with the Holy Spirit and fire unto your God.

(Matthew 3:11)

The Holy Spirit descended in bodily form like a dove upon him, and a voice came from heaven which said, "This is my beloved Son, in whom I am well pleased." (John 2:19)

The Holy Spirit is the spirit of God the Son. The energy of God the Son descends from God the Father, and during the baptism of the soul, your carnal mind will change to Christ's mind. Heaven, the plane of the spirits, the holiest place of the I Am that I Am, the place of the ascended masters.

For Christ has not entered the holy places made with hands, but into heaven itself now to appear in the presence of God for us all.

(Hebrews 9:24)

Our hearts, minds, and conscience are the dwelling place of God. The light that shines in the darkness the (add "that") darkness could not overcome. The sins of the flesh create darkness, moving us further away from God's light. Though your sins be as scarlet, they shall be as white as snow; though they be red like crimson, they shall be as wool, says the Lord. Whatever we do, our ability to return to God is always there; the light and breath of God continue inside us.

Let this mind be in you which was also in Christ Jesus.

(Philippians 2:5)

When we talk about mind and heart, we are speaking about God and human—our thoughts and feelings, actions (plural), good and evil. God's spirit makes our heart beat. Where are you when it comes to the truth and falsehood (or "false")? God's will or human will? We use God's energy in all the things that we do—teaching in the classroom, flying an airplane, doing sports, attending to patients in the hospital, dancing and singing, serving Mass (capitalize), providing security, and all work and duties. He is omnipresent and the source of life. Yes, God does all this work through us humans. We serve one another, carrying out His (capitalized) rules and instructions.

When we don't follow God's order to do our work and duties, things go wrong, and it affects people. We are developing and advancing in science and technology, learning about things around us: near and far galaxies, planets, heaven, the earth, the sky, space, the moon, Mars, stars, Jupiter, the sun, and the cosmos. We are at the beginning stages (or "stage") of our mission, exploring the universe, hoping to find and see what exists out there—what living beings they are and in what form, mineral resources, habitable and sustainable planets, another Earth (capitalized) that is created by God, somewhere in the universe, in our galaxy or in another galaxy that is inhabited by living beings having physical and divine aspects.

The Lord God knows that, with time, humans will come searching. Consider the distance between galaxies; consider the law of creation and human DNA. Already we have started the journey. If indeed life exists, I am sure it does, probably in another galaxy. The universe is big and endless for us humans to be in it alone. God the Creator, with all His (capitalized) power, wisdom, and love, will not leave the rest of the galaxy and planets void and empty. If life does exist in another galaxy, can we get there? Could they have a different God other than ours? Is it forbidden, or is it allowed that we humans see them and they see us? Will they know who we are? Would we know who they are? For those who will go, if they get there, will they survive? Will they return back to earth? Going to nearby planets within our galaxy is a big task. For humans going out of our galaxy to another galaxy, this will require the will, guidance, and leadership of God and divine intervention. Man is made with the soil of the earth and the breath of God; so we are habitable and adaptable to earth and its gravity. We have the breath of God, but we are not made with the soil of another planet. God the Creator is with us; He (capitalized) knows about rockets and satellites. He placed us here. Like Elijah, Jesus Christ could have just transfigured and ascended into heaven, but He (capitalized) chose to visit us and spend time with us, his children. He loves us and died on the cross for us. Elijah did not ascend into heaven with a man-made machine but with a divine machine made in heaven.

Humans are physical and spiritual. Will the Creator reveal to us humans (or "us") and lead us to outer planets out there in the universe that are inhabited by visible beings? There are spiritual beings around us here on planet earth. Yes, we are in time and space that we do not see; we see what God allows us to see. If it's God's plan, He will guard and lead us there. In this crucial mission to the unknown world, it will be good to seek God and include in the crew a man of God. From Adam, Eve, Noah, and Abraham to now and tomorrow, He is the Maker and the Creator. Where He wants us to go, there He will lead us. First, the Creator loves us; and we must love the Creator with our heart, mind, and soul, and learn to love and live in peace with one another. We must stop evil and overcome these limitations that make us human. As we learn and grow in His knowledge—humanly and spiritually—we will advance toward His goals and plans.

We will learn physically and spiritually as we go through this journey of the wilderness of life. The earth is the human home, the material world, the physical world, the land of the living, for all creatures. The flesh, the mortal aspect of humans (or "the human") with all its desires and emotional needs and wants, is corrupt and sometimes blind in its actions and movements, asking for forgiveness. The energy of God the Father should be used correctly. Every thought and deed comes from our minds.

In my Father's house, there are many mansions. Anger, hate, greed, evil, and crime are not treasures. Help, kindness, love, and peace—joy for fellow humans—these are the treasures you can store up in the mansion above to please God. Misusing the energy of God causes sin, stress, crisis, crime, suffering, sickness, evil, separation from God, and pollution of the Earth's atmosphere. Through the love, grace, and mercy of God, and our forgiveness and repentance toward one another, our sins are washed away continuously.

Lord Jesus said, "The harvest truly is plentiful, but the laborers are few." (Matthew 9:37)

The human population will continue to grow, and so will the demand for their needs. The Lord said to Peter, "Feed my lambs; feed my sheep." (John 21:15)

God needs laborers on earth; He gave us different talents to help and provide for one another. He uses us to distribute His resources to one another. Use your talents and gifts to make life better for you and others. Do not destroy, kill, or contaminate God's work; make it a better place for you and all. People will not only benefit from your goodness; it will change them and inspire them.

Chapter 8

GOD THROWS AWAY THE BAD FRUITS

And have no fellowship with the unfruitful works of darkness that are done by them in secret.

(Ephesians 5:11)

They shall be thrown out in silence, said the Lord God. We would rather expose them, for it is shameful even to speak of those things which they do.

(Amos 8:3–4)

Whoever believes and is baptized will be saved, but whoever does not believe will be condemned. And these signs will accompany those who believe: In my name, they will drive out demons; they will speak in new tongues; they will pick up snakes with their hands; and when they drink deadly poison, it will not hurt them at all. They will place their hands on sick people, and they will get well.

(Mark 16:16–18)

As Moses lifted up the serpent in the wilderness, so must the Son of Man be lifted up, that whoever believes in him should not perish but have eternal life.

(John 3:14–15)

Just as the Israelites in the wilderness were safe from the bite of the serpent by looking up to the bronze serpent, Jesus Christ is raised, ascended into heaven by God the Father, and those who look up to him for their sins shall be saved. Jesus Christ was lifted up, and he ascended into the highest heaven. The power of light—the cross of Jesus Christ—is to save and protect humanity; the power of darkness—the devil—is lesser, to kill and destroy.

Their identity is always revealed when the angel of the Lord confronts them—the wolf that goes after the sheep and the hawk that chases away the hen and goes after the chickens. They are bad fruits, anti-Christ; God shall throw them away.

Chapter 9

CLIMB UP TO GOD

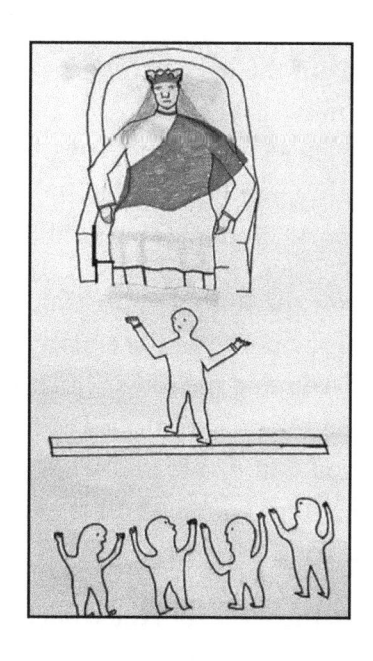

He who dwells in the secret place of the Most High shall abide under the shadow of the Almighty. I will set him on high because he has known my name. He shall call upon me, and I will answer him; I will be with him in trouble. I will deliver him and honor him. He prepares a table before me in the presence of my enemies in the face of the evil ones and the power of darkness.

(Psalm 91)

You will step up to the Lord God for protection; the evil one cannot reach you. Every sickness you will drop at the table of our Lord Jesus Christ. And in the name of our Lord Jesus Christ of

Nazareth, the Star of Bethlehem, the enemy will be defeated, and its identity will be revealed.

If you had known me, you should have known my Father also; and from henceforth you know him and have seen him. You told me so; I believe you, Lord. I am in my Father, and you in me, and I in you.

(John 14:7)

You told me so, "I am the light of the world. He that follows me will not walk in darkness." You told me so, and I believe you, Lord. Do not be afraid; be of good courage, and let not your heart be troubled. You believe in God; believe also in me. Be of good cheer. I have overcome the world. You told me so, and I believe you, Lord.

"Behold, I give you the authority to trample on serpents and scorpions and over all the power of the enemy, and nothing shall by any means hurt you." You told me so; you all are made in the image of God. Love your neighbor as yourself. Do not worry about what you will wear, what you will drink, and what you will eat, for your heavenly Father knows that you need all these things. You told me so, and I believe You, Lord.

"As Moses lifted up the serpent in the wilderness, so must the Son of Man be lifted up, and those who look up to him shall be saved." You told me so. "Greater is he that is in you than he that is in the world." You told me so, and I believe You, Lord.

The knowledge of good and evil is the independence and free will self-control that God gave to Adam and Eve. It is what makes us human, a balancing force. Every human that comes into this world possesses it. How we will use it and what we do with it is what matters. We are God's children; He created us and crowned us with honor and glory and gave us control over all the work of His hand.

In addition, we have the power and the knowledge from God to build and make good things for our better living; there's no need for us to do evil. All things that humans have done and all things that we are doing today result from the knowledge of good and evil. Everything is created for our own purpose; we use them, and we learn from them.

We are getting carried away by worldly things and not spending time to think about the source of all these things. Humans are different and do things differently, but others want you to do things their own way. Sometimes you win; sometimes you lose, and no one wants to lose.

We humans are like God; He made us in His image. The issue is humans challenge God all the time. We know right from wrong but choose to do wrong and disobey God. Jesus Christ reigns forever, rules forever, and lives forever; that is true. What is also true is that Jesus Christ is the Son of God the Father, and through Him, He made man.

Chapter 10

Baptism of the Soul

"The Trinity consists of God the Father above, God the Son in the middle, and God the Holy Spirit below. God the Father is the Creator; God the Son is the Preserver; and God the Holy Spirit is the spirit of God within us, allowing the human soul to ascend and rise. The human soul is the image of God in humanity, while the soul and the flesh are the consumer and the destroyer. The firstborn said to his father, "These many years do I serve thee; you did not give me a goat that I might make merry. But as soon as this thy son came, who hath devoured thy living, the consumer and the destroyer, you killed the fatted calf." The father replied, "Thy younger brother was dead and is alive again; he was lost and is found. You are my first son; thou art ever with me, and all that I have is thine."

Now that the soul, the prodigal son, has risen to the Christ self, the Holy Spirit, the divine child, and has returned to God the Father, he should stop doing evil and start doing good, supporting the elder brother, the firstborn, and serving God the Father. We pray, we praise God, we give glory to the Lord, yet we continue to sin again and again: wars, killing, greed, corruption, environmental destruction, contamination of wildlife, and all sorts of evil persist."

Remember, the firstborn son is in the field working and serving God the Father. The more evil we do, the more sins we commit, and the more work we create for the firstborn. We all should join the firstborn, Jesus Christ, and work together for God the Father.

The soul partakes in the divine needs of God and in the physical needs of humanity. The soul, the prodigal son who has returned home to the Father, is a brother to God the Son. The human flesh, the visible physical aspect of humanity, is also a spirit and serves as the earthly vessel. They combine and function together.

The soul, the immortal aspect of humanity, is given independence and free will to obey the Holy Spirit and the human spirit. When we do well, we draw closer to God; when we do evil, we move away from Him. Man is made of the breath of God and all things on earth.

The human flesh is mortal, subject to barriers and the law of gravity; the soul, the immortal aspect of man, is the superman angel without barriers and not subject to gravity. Often, whether good or bad, the soul follows the desires of the human spirit and the flesh. As the soul rises, the light and energy of God fill the body. As the soul becomes corrupted, the light and energy of God decrease.

The level to which the soul gravitates toward the physical, and the beast toward the pit, is uncertain. Most often, through the mercy and forgiveness of God, they are rescued. The baptism of the flesh with water is physical, while the baptism of the soul with the Holy Spirit and Holy Ghost fire is divine and spiritual. The voice of him that crieth in the wilderness says, "Prepare ye the way of the Lord; make straight in the desert a highway for our God. Every valley shall be exalted, and every mountain and hill shall be made low; the crooked shall be made straight, and the rough places plain."

And the glory of the Lord shall be revealed, and all flesh shall see it together; for the mouth of the Lord hath spoken it. That which is born of the flesh is flesh, and that which is born of the Spirit is spirit (John 3:6).

"I indeed baptize you with water unto repentance to receive Jesus Christ. Jesus Christ wills to baptize you with the Holy Spirit and Holy Ghost. Behold, I send my messenger, and he will prepare the way before me. And the Lord God that you seek will suddenly come to His temple. And who can stand when He appears? For He is like a refiner's fire and like a launderer's soap" (Malachi 3:1-3).

Messengers of God are on earth, baptizing humans with holy water to bring them to Jesus Christ. Jesus Christ will baptize them with the Holy Spirit and Holy Ghost fire. To their God, the Holy Spirit will come to you, take control of you, and transform your mind from a carnal mind to a Christ mind.

In the nighttime, in the bedroom, it was quiet and peaceful. I was reading the book of John about the arrest of Jesus Christ in the garden of Gethsemane. They went to a place called Gethsemane, and Jesus said to his disciples, "Sit here while I pray" (Mark 14:32). He took with him Peter, James, and John, and began to be sore amazed and very heavy. He said unto them, "My soul is exceeding sorrowful unto death; stay here and watch." He went forward a little, fell on the ground, and prayed that, if it were possible, the hour might pass from him. He said, "Abba, Father, all things are possible unto Thee; take away this cup from me. Nevertheless, not what I will, but Your will be done. For this I came into the world." He said to Pilate, "You don't have power over me unless it were given to you from above. I have authority to lay it down and authority to take it up again. I give it up willingly. No man takes it from me."

Judas, then, having received a band of men and officers from the chief priests and Pharisees, came there with lanterns, torches, and weapons. Jesus, therefore, knowing all things that should come upon him, went forth and said unto them, "Whom seek ye?" They answered him, "Jesus of Nazareth." Jesus said unto them, "I am he." And Judas, who betrayed him, stood with them. As soon as he had said unto them, "I am he," they went backward and fell to the ground. Then he asked them again, "Whom seek ye?" And they said, "Jesus of Nazareth." "I have told you that I am he; if it is me you want, let these go.

Osenon Tony lay in bed, sorrow and sadness filling his whole body, mind, and soul at the suffering and death of Jesus Christ. He felt some movement inside his heart; something shifted and turned around 180 degrees. Silently and smoothly, he sensed the movement of the Holy Spirit of God. He groaned and saw two reptile-like creatures, one chasing the other and crawling on the wall. One was smashed and killed, while the other vanished from sight. He was afraid and cried out, "Oh my God, they killed Jesus Christ." From one of the four corners of the room, he heard a voice: "Yes, I am your God." He stared in the direction from which the voice came, and within himself he said, "No fire, no burning bush." He fell into a deep sleep, unsure if he was alive or dead.

Then a bright, dazzling window opened up, filled with winds and beams of light. Everything was blown away except him, standing in Christ, within the midst of the beam of light, his face turned upward. A woman ran across in a flash. Then, in the sky, he saw burning stars lining up and coming from opposite directions, right and left, moving at high speed. One by one, the stars collided in the sky with a huge explosion that illuminated the entire sky. Standing below, I faced upward, shouting loudly and repeatedly, "Jesus Christ of Nazareth, the Star of Bethlehem.

The collision of the stars continued, forming many rings of fire cycles, from the center to the outer ring. All began through the center ring, burning, brightening, and lighting up the entire sky. Below the colliding stars stood a large burning cross, both vertical and horizontal. Beneath the burning cross was me. Everything was ablaze—sparks and beams of light from the colliding stars and from the cross—all coming down on me.

I woke up the next day with sparks and flashes of fire in my eyes, feeling a burning sensation all over my body; it was visible but not painful. A few days later, the burns on my body were gone.

Osenon Tony knows he has encountered the divine. What had happened that fateful night? He prayed and called on to God. He called on to Jesus Christ. They heard him and answered him, and they came. I thank God the Father. I thank God the Son, Jesus Christ of Nazareth, the star of Bethlehem. I thank the Holy Spirit; they led me through safely, and I survived it all. All glory and honor is yours forever and ever. Amen. Lord Jesus Christ, Son of God, you have fought and won the battle for us. All over the world, your children, sons and daughters of God, are increasing, multiplying, and returning to you every day. Lord, you visited and spent some time with us, our God in human flesh and blood. You taught us, you healed us, you cured us, you blessed us, you prayed for us, and you fed us. Thank you. The blind see, the deaf hear, the sick healed, the deformed restored, and the dead rise. You healed them all that were brought to you, and none went away unhealed. Thank you. You died on the cross for us, our sins, our pain, our sickness, and our death. You took them from us; you paid the price of our sins when you died on the cross for us. Thank you. Lord, you are always in our heart; you are always in our mind. You love us, and we love you too. Your pain, your sorrow, your tears, your passion, your agony, your arrest in the garden of Gethsemane, your judgment, your suffering, your crucifixion on the cross—we felt it. Lord Jesus Christ, you ascended into heaven for us, and you are seated at the right hand of God the Father Almighty. I believe in you, Lamb of God, who was sacrificed for the sins of the world. Have mercy on me; see me and hear me in my prayer, in my tears, in my pain, in my sickness, and in my agony. I cry up to you. My thoughts, my feelings, and my soul, through thy Holy Spirit of God in me, I seek, I ask, I knock, and call up unto you. Abba, hear me, see me, answer my call, open the window of heaven for me, come into my heart, come into my mind, send thy light, send thy Holy Ghost fire down unto me, baptize me, baptize my soul unto my God, and let a new baby Christ be born in heaven unto you today. Angels are rejoicing in heaven; glory be to God, our heavenly Father. Alleluia! Amen. When this happens, you are being baptized with the Holy Spirit and Holy Ghost fire by Jesus Christ. Reunited with your God, access to heaven is granted. You put on a new self. Your old self is dead. The barrier, the separation between you and your God, between you and heaven, is removed. Christ is born, and God will speak to you; you will grow up spiritually. You are a Christ in the making. Praise God! Alleluia! Amen.

Chapter 11

COVER THE GRAVE THE ENEMY DUG

They that wait upon the Lord shall renew their strength (Isaiah 40:31). They shall mount up with wings like eagles; they shall run and not be weary, and they shall walk and not faint. I will ransom them from the power of the grave; I will redeem them from death. Who is seeking the living among the dead?

Jesus Christ lives, and you live also. Every crooked place shall be made straight, and every rough edge shall be smoothed. The Lord your God is He who goes with you to fight for you against your enemies. "Believe in God; also believe in me." With the Holy Spirit of God in you and our Savior, Jesus Christ of Nazareth, the Star of Bethlehem, your soul—the Holy Spirit, your angel—will soar into space, locate the grave that the enemy has dug, and cover it up. Every weapon and every device of the enemy will not prosper. The enemy is defeated, and through the mercy of our Lord Jesus Christ, the enemy is saved from going down into the grave that he dug. God formed man out of the dust of the ground and breathed into his nostrils the breath of life, and man became a living soul. And the Lord said, "My spirit shall not strive with man forever, for he is indeed flesh; his days shall be one hundred and twenty years" (Genesis 6:3).

Man is made from both the soil of the earth and the breath of God. My spirit shall not strive with man and shall not compete with man forever, for he is indeed flesh. The flesh is the temple of God, the physical body through which we feel, see, and experience the world. The human body is a mixture of everything that the earth and Heaven are made of; we are earthly and heavenly beings. He created the earth pure and clean, which is being corrupted by our impure thoughts, feelings, and actions. God is merciful, loving, and forgiving.

We are the apple of His eye—smart or foolish, rich or poor, tall or short, black or white, old or young. We have different cultures, languages, and religions; but He loves us all.

Angels are divine, higher beings, a part of you that will fight and defeat the devil. The devil is the anti-Christ. Some people, through the witchcraft power of darkness, use all sources of knowledge—such as fear, gifts, and attraction—to deceive God's children, getting them to lower their spiritual defenses, and then carry out their evil intentions to kill, harm, and destroy.

Jesus Christ issued this to us: "Behold, I give you the power to tread on serpents and scorpions and over all the powers of the enemy, and nothing shall by any means hurt you. Let not your heart be troubled, nor let it be afraid. I am with you always, anywhere, anytime.

God is omnipresent, both finite and infinite; He is in everything. He is everywhere—in you, in Heaven, on earth, in the sea, in water, in the sky, in storms, in rain, in floods, in earthquakes, in volcanoes, in snow, in fire, in space, in nights and days, when asleep or awake, in food, in water, in mountains, in pits, in caves, in oceans, in rivers, and in lakes. God made Heaven and earth; He created every living creature that dwells in you. He made them and brought them to Adam, and whatsoever Adam named them, that was their name. He is with you, whether rich or poor. He is with you in sickness and in good health. He is with you in wars, battles, and dangers. He is with you everywhere, anywhere, anytime. He is with you. We thank You, Lord.

There is plenty of everything for everyone. Be peaceful. Don't commit evil for anything. There is more from the source. God is the source. He will provide more. Thank Him always for His mercy.

Angels are divine, crystal-white heavenly beings. Devils are dark beings from hell. Two of the trees in the Garden of Eden are the tree of the knowledge of good and evil and the tree of life; both trees bear fruit: the heavenly tree and the earthly tree.

God is our Father; we are God's children. He created planet Earth and placed in it all our needs. Behold, the man has become as one of us, knowing good and evil. Though we are humans, as children of God, He gave us the knowledge to create good things and the knowledge to destroy the bad things that we humans created, not the things that God created.

Yet, humans continue to kill and destroy the good things created by God. Only God has the full and permanent power to create, destroy, and remove.

In the book of Hebrews, Moses's offering brought a temporary solution. God incarnated Jesus Christ as human flesh and blood, born of the Virgin Mary; He experienced and destroyed death.

You have the first death and the second death. The first death is natural and is not a spiritual death. The second death is a spiritual death, a punishment.

Christ is alive; if Christ is in you, your spirit is alive also for eternity. He lived among us. His death on the cross frees us from sin and opens the window of heaven, granting us permanent access directly to God and directly to heaven.

He will continue to renew us from our sins until we become obedient, holy, and peaceful in a world full of love and mercy—no anger, no hate, no evil, no sin, no war, no sickness, no death.

Chapter 12

The Art of Healing

"Rejects him who sent." The seventy-two returned with joy and said, "LORD, even the demons submit to us in your name." He replied, "I saw Satan fall like lightning from heaven. I have given you authority to trample on snakes and scorpions and to overcome all the power of the enemy; nothing shall, by any means, harm you. However, do not rejoice that the spirits submit to you, but rejoice that your names are written in heaven. Let it be done on earth as it is done in heaven.

"I can of my own self do nothing: as I hear, I judge, and my judgment is just because I seek not my own will but the will of the Father who has sent me. If any man will do his will, he shall know of the doctrine, whether it be of God or whether I speak of myself.

Then said Jesus unto them, "When you have lifted up the Son of Man, then you shall know that I am He; you will know God, and that I do nothing of myself; but as my Father has taught me, I speak these things. And He who sent me is with me; the Father has not left me alone, for I do always those things that please Him. The words that I speak unto you, I speak not of myself; but the Father that dwelleth in me, He doeth the works.

Afterward, Jesus found him in the temple and said unto him, "Behold, thou art made whole; sin no more, lest a worse thing come unto thee. Verily, verily, I say unto you, the Son can do nothing of Himself but what He sees the Father do; for what things soever... "Whoever listens to you listens to me; whoever rejects you rejects me; but whoever rejects me."

In the name of Jesus Christ of Nazareth, the Star of Bethlehem, the evil unclean demon spirit is defeated and driven out of me in heaven and on earth. The Holy Spirit of God is now in control of my life. He keeps me holy and clean. Lord, have mercy on my son, for he is lunatic and sore vexed; for oftentimes he falls into the fire (Matthew 17:15) and often into the water.

Verily, verily, I say unto you, he that believeth on me, the works that I do shall he do also; and greater works than these shall he do because I go unto my Father. And I brought him to thy disciples, and they could not cure him. Bring him hither to me. And Jesus rebuked the devil, and he departed out of him; and the child was cured from that very hour.

Then came the disciples to Jesus apart and said, "Why could we not cast him out?" And Jesus said unto them, "Because of your unbelief; for verily I say unto you, if ye have faith as a grain of mustard seed, ye shall say unto this mountain, "Remove hence to yonder place," and it shall remove; and nothing shall be impossible unto you. Howbeit this kind goeth not out but by prayer and fasting. What have we to do with you, Christ, the Son of God?"

What have I to do with thee, Jesus, thou Son of the highest God? I adjure thee by God that thou torment me not." For he said unto him, "Come out of the man, thou unclean spirit." And he asked him, "What is thy name?" And he answered, saying, "My name is Legion, for we are many." And he besought him much that he would not send them away out of the country.

Now there was nigh unto the mountains a great herd of swine feeding. And all the devils besought him, saying, "Send us into the swine that we may enter into them." And forthwith Jesus gave them leave. And the unclean spirits went out and entered into the swine; and the herd ran violently down a steep place into the sea (they were about two thousand) and were choked in the sea.

Demons and unclean spirits have to seek permission from God in the realm of the spirits; they are bound from entering into humans and other living things unless they open up and allow them in. What are demons, and how do they enter people? First, let's read these verses from the Bible.

"For the flesh lusteth against the Spirit, and the Spirit against the flesh; and these are contrary the one to the other, so that ye cannot do the things that ye would. But if ye be led of the Spirit, ye are not under the law. Now the works of the flesh are manifest, which are these: Adultery, fornication, uncleanness, lasciviousness, idolatry, witchcraft, hatred, variance, emulations, wrath, strife, seditions, heresies, envying, murders, drunkenness, reveling, and such like; of the which I tell you before, as I have also told you in time past, that they which do such things shall not inherit the kingdom of God.

But the fruit of the Spirit is love, joy, peace, longsuffering, gentleness, goodness, faith, meekness, and temperance (Galatians 5:22–23). People are often open-minded; they don't plan evil, nor do they expect evil to be planned against them. Yes, the Holy Spirit of God is within you. He knows and sees the thoughts and spirits of others. Jesus Christ told the man, "Behold, thou art made whole. Sin no more." You can either listen to the Holy Spirit of God or to the human spirit.

When the unclean spirit has gone out of a person, it walks through dry places, seeking rest and finding none. Then it says, "I will return to my house from whence I came." And when it comes, it finds it empty, swept, and garnished. Then it goes and takes with itself seven other spirits more wicked than itself, and they enter in and dwell there; and the last state of that person is worse than the first (Matthew 12:43–45).

After the demon was driven out, the person did not allow Christ's Holy Spirit to take control. Absent the Holy Spirit, the demon returned and found the house empty. God is our Father; He made us. The Devil did not create us but seeks to possess us, caring little for how many he harms in pursuit of his agenda: world wars, weapons of mass destruction, genocide, toxicity, and radiation. Return to God, accept the Savior Jesus Christ, repent, and sin no more. Some humans are influenced by demonic forces and are capable of casting evil and harmful spells on their unsuspecting fellow humans.

And all the devils besought him, saying, "Send us into the swine, that we may enter into them." The demon is a homeless spirit. "What have I to do with thee, Jesus, thou Son of the highest God?" (Mark 5:12)

When Jesus Christ lives in you, there will be no room in your life for homeless demons; they will not even dare to come nearby.

We don't know where sickness and illness come from. It's very sad and touching to see fellow humans sick, ill, and in pain. How did it start? Did it arise from our ways of life, the things we eat, our actions, or the environment in which we live? What can we do to completely eradicate all sickness and illness that affect us in different ways and sometimes cause death?

What can we humans do to live happily, healthily, and free from sickness? That is a question everyone is asking, and the answer is something everyone wants to know. The key to healing is your love for God and deep compassion for the condition of others. Believe in God, believe in Jesus Christ, and have faith in yourself. First, we should heal ourselves before we can heal others.

God gave us free will. All have sinned and come short of the glory of God. We have culture, human laws, and God's laws. We know that many of the things we consume and many of our actions are harmful to our health and against God's will, yet we choose to continue doing them. We become addicted, and they become a way of life.

Yes, God gave us free will. We have the knowledge of good and evil. We have eaten from the tree of life. We are like God, possessing the knowledge of both divinity and humanity. He allows us full control. Yes, He is our Father, rich in everything. He wants us to live happily and joyfully, free from evil and sickness.

He wants us to learn, explore, discover, create excitement, and preserve His resources. He doesn't want us to engage in harmful behaviors. Who will guard you from the evil one, from unclean spirits and demons? He is there to keep you alive, to guard, and to protect you.

Have you met Jesus Christ of Nazareth, the Star of Bethlehem? He is the beloved Son of God; through Him, everything was made and created. He is the best Father and the best friend one can ever have. He came into the world as God in physical human form and lived among us so that you might live and not die, and so that you should not be sick. He came to free us and protect us from all evil forces.

He is our heavenly Father. He loves you, and you should love Him too with all your mind, heart, and soul. He is very compassionate. He forgives sins, raises the dead, heals the sick, gives sight to the blind, hearing to the deaf, and restoration to the deformed.

Any person who wants to harm or kill another human is an anti-Christ, an enemy of God. God performs many wonders. He strengthens you physically and spiritually, giving you the ability to heal and cure yourself and to heal others. He prevents evil, sickness, and illness from reaching you. He sees them before you do, stops them, shows you signs, and speaks to you. Then you know He has seen them and will join you to fight, defeat the devil, cure you, and flush them out of your body, His temple.

Jesus Christ knows and sees all things. Go to Him; He will heal you. His angels will pull you out of the pit of death and brush away all the dust from your body. God is continuously protecting and healing us, and we should do our part to work with Him to protect His temple—your body.

You will move away from your enemy to the table of the Lord God for safety. Your sickness, your worries, and your fears—you will drop them at the table of our Lord God. He will take them from you, heal you, and set you free. Amen.

Chapter 13

CHRIST LABORERS

Basic essential needs for one's neighbor provide for me. All will live well in light and in truth.

The country belongs to the people. When the people are idle, the country is idle; when the people are working, the country is working. The country doesn't build people; people build the country.

Developed countries have advanced greatly in religion and science; they manufacture everything and produce the basic necessities for a better life. Underdeveloped countries are heavily focused on religion and agriculture but lag behind in science, technology, and manufacturing.

There are many colleges and universities in these countries. The children are very intelligent and well-educated, excelling in all subjects. After graduation, the majority of them find work, but there are few jobs due to the limited number of factories and industries. They maintain a low standard of living, depending on foreign technology and locally produced goods.

The earth is rich in mineral resources, and every country in the world has enough of them. These minerals are processed and used to produce the essential items and components that humans depend on. Basic necessities—food, water, sanitation, housing, drainage systems, security, electricity, roads, transportation, and health care—are lacking in developing countries.

Jesus Christ said to you all, "Love your neighbor as yourself." That is the golden rule: God loves and cares for us. He has given us all the natural resources—water, air, fire, fruit, herbs, and more—freely. Do unto others as you would like others to do unto you. Walk in the light of Christ. The primary concern should be to ensure a better life for humanity.

Jesus Christ said, "I am the light of the world. He that follows me shall not walk in darkness."

Truly, these times of ignorance God overlooked, but now commands all humans everywhere to repent and obey the golden rule (Acts 17:30).

The golden rule should be obeyed: do unto others as you would have them do unto you. In John 21, Jesus Christ said to Peter, "Feed my lambs, feed my sheep." In Matthew 9:37-38, it is written that the harvest is plentiful, but the laborers are few. Jesus Christ is the Lamb of God, pure and sinless; He takes away the sins of the world and redeems us from our sins.

Lambs and sheep: there is a difference between lambs and sheep; all we like sheep have gone astray. Peter is the leader of the apostles. Just as Jesus Christ loves us, He cares for, protects, and provides for us, including His apostles. He handed over the responsibility to Peter to care for, protect, and provide for the people.

Sheep and lambs represent both the physical and the spiritual. The sheep are the people, and the lamb represents the Holy Spirit—Christ in us, pure, innocent, and sinless. It is okay to have leaders—heads of churches, religious leaders, reverend fathers, pastors, elected officials, and company owners. All should care for, protect, and provide for the people. They should serve the people they represent and perform the work they are appointed to do.

The development of every area of the country creates jobs for its people. In every state and province, we should set up factories to produce and manufacture necessary goods. Everyone should work together to overcome the stack of erroneous mistakes: greed and corruption that have kept development lagging in developing countries.

Ungodliness, greed, corruption, inequality, disrespect, abandonment, and neglect of the people—neglect of the country—will never bring about the solutions urgently needed for development. These practices cause hardship, poverty, suffering, disorganization, unemployment, crime, and underdevelopment.

How long will this continue? Who will bring about change: the leaders or the people? As the population grows, the demands grow. What is lacking is the country we are supposed to build but have not built, and the jobs we are supposed to create but have not created. The people we are supposed to care for have not been cared for.

Advance planning and job creation is a continuous process. Indeed, all will be rich when your country is developed, and great when your country is great. You will be praised and respected.

Advance planning and job creation are continuous processes. Indeed, all will be rich when your country is developed, and great when your country is great. You will be praised and respected.

The dragon stood in front of the woman who was about to give birth, so that it might devour her child the moment he was born. She gave birth to a son, a male child, who will rule all the nations with an iron scepter, and her child was snatched up to God and to His throne. The woman fled into the wilderness to a place prepared for her by God. (Revelation 12:1–6)

He seized the dragon, that ancient serpent, who is the devil or Satan, and bound him for a thousand years. He threw him into the Abyss and locked and sealed it over him to keep him from deceiving the nations anymore until the thousand years were ended.

After that, he must be set free for a short time. (Revelation 20:2–7)

And when the dragon saw that he was cast down to the earth, he persecuted the woman who brought forth the male child. And to the woman were given two wings of a great eagle, so that she might fly into the wilderness. (Revelation 12:13–15) The angel of the Lord appeared to Joseph in a dream, saying, "Arise, and take the young child and his mother, and flee into Egypt."

In the book of Matthew, Herod beheaded John the Baptist. We all know that God came to visit us as a human. Satan has many names: Lucifer, devil, tempter. He is a spirit who lives beyond the physical, tempting humans through their carnal minds. When Jesus Christ was tempted, He rebuked the devil, saying, "Get away from me."

In the ancient Roman Empire, Nero's image appeared on Roman coins. Today, all over the world, there are images of people appearing on coins and currency. Human work should be limited to four days a week; Friday, Saturday, and Sunday should be off days. We are working too hard and not getting enough rest. Stress, weakness, and illness are on the rise. There is plenty of everything for everyone.

Doing well brings joy, happiness, peace of mind, good health, and a good life, while evil brings sickness, horror, stress, and sadness. God is good. Everything He made and created is good. Don't be afraid. Do not let your heart be troubled, for God, who made all things, lives in you.

Praise God. Any attack against you is an attack against God and His Son, Jesus Christ. Angels are heavenly beings; humans are earthly beings. Devils represent the dark and evil side of human beings.

Humans are like God, but we are not equal to God. Storms come in various forms: natural storms such as hurricanes, tsunamis, snowstorms, earthquakes, heavy rain, and overflowing rivers. The wind can be peaceful, friendly, and invisible; at times, it can also be unfriendly, violent, and destructive. Nothing stands in its way. Trees and houses are thrown down, and its effects can be seen by human eyes.

Human-related storms include sickness and illness, such as strokes, heart attacks, cancer, kidney failure, lung infections, and so on. In both cases, sometimes life is lost and property is damaged. God gave us the knowledge of good and evil—the ability to know what is right and what is wrong. But God wants us to act according to His will, rather than our own. Good and evil are what make us human. We work toward perfection as the life cycle continues by doing things God's way.

God is light. God is truth. He resides in our hearts, and we are judged by our thoughts, decisions, and actions. Sometimes the things we do contribute to natural storms: long underground tunnels, drilling holes to the core of the earth in search of mineral resources, pollution of the atmosphere, and environmental contamination through deforestation and urbanization. Do not judge; God the Father is righteous, and humans continuously do things that are wrong. The Son of God, Jesus Christ, judges us all; He knows the spirit of man and the spirit of God. First, God is there to guide us when we rise and catch us when we fall; we should listen to His voice. The first Adam represents the body, mind, and soul; the second Adam is the Holy Spirit. The tree of life in the midst of the Garden of Eden is a savior tree, the Holy Spirit. His teachings are alive in us. God is our Father; we are His children, and He is teaching us His ways.

I am made in the image of God, and all are made in the image of God; I see them, and they see me, dead or alive. I retain their image, and they retain the image of me. I still remember them. What was said many years ago is alive in me. You may not like the way the other person drives his car; the thing is, you cannot drive two cars at the same time. Drive your own car safely, mind your driving, and don't be distracted, angry, or furious, losing control over how someone else drives his car.

God is always there for you. With God, you will not be dead, for He is alive to supply your breath. When you are lonely, He will comfort you. You will not be cold; His fire will warm you. You will not be dry, for His crystal river of water will flow through you completely. You will not be hungry, for His Word will fill you. He fills the earth with herbs, fruits, and seeds. You will not be lost, for He created heaven and earth, and He is everywhere.

Lord God, Father, give me life, love me, care for me, guard me, protect me, provide for me, teach me, lead me, and direct me; have mercy on me. Your knowledge is vast within my body. I thank You for all these wonderful gifts You have given us. Praise be Your name forever and ever. Amen.

"I am the way, the truth, and the life; no man comes unto the Father but by me." (John 14:6)

Jesus Christ is the Alpha and the Omega, the beginning and the end of creation, the breath of life, the second Adam, the life-giving Spirit through whom Adam and Eve were made. And through Jesus Christ, we can all eat of the tree of life and return to God the Father. The Word was made flesh. "Let there be light," and it was so that everything that came into existence came through His spoken Word.

Greater is He that is in you than he that is in the world. You told me so, and I believe You, Lord.

Chapter 14

SONGS AND PRAYERS

Song 1

If you had known me, you should have known my Father also;
and from henceforth you know Him and have seen Him.
You told me so; I believe You, Lord.
I am in my Father, and you in me, and I in you.
In Jesus's name, in Jesus's name, in Jesus's name I pray.
I pray, I pray, I pray in Jesus's name, I pray. Alleluia!
I pray, Hosanna in the highest I pray. Amen.
Jesus Christ of Nazareth, the Star of Bethlehem,
I am in your care; watch over me.
In Jesus's name I pray, Alleluia!
I pray, Hosanna in the highest I pray. Amen.
My Lord, my Lord, on the cross you set me free from my sins and death.
In Jesus's name I pray, Alleluia! I pray, Hosanna in the highest I pray.
Amen.
He guards me up the ladder when I rise and catches me when I fall.
In Jesus's name I pray, Alleluia! I pray, Hosanna in the highest I pray.
Amen.
He strengthens me when I am weak.
In Jesus's name I pray, Alleluia!
I pray, Hosanna in the highest I pray. Amen.
You are always in my heart, Jesus;
you are always in my mind, Jesus.
I am alive, I am free; I thank You, Father.
In Jesus's name I pray, Alleluia!
I pray, Hosanna in the highest I pray. Amen.

Song 2

You told me so; I believe You, Lord.
"I am the light of the world.
He that follows me will not walk in darkness."
You told me so; I believe You, Lord.
"Do not be afraid. Be of good courage;
let not your heart be troubled."
You told me so; I believe You, Lord.
"Believe in God; believe also in me.
Be of good cheer. I have overcome the world."
You told me so; I believe You, Lord.
"Behold, I give you the authority to trample
on serpents and scorpions and over all the power of the enemy,
and nothing shall by any means hurt you."
You told me so; I believe You, Lord.
"Do unto others what you would want others to do unto you.
Love your neighbor as yourself."
You told me so; I believe You, Lord.
"Do not worry about what you will wear,
what you will drink, and what you will eat,
for your heavenly Father knows that you need all these things."
You told me so; I believe You, Lord.
"As Moses lifted up the serpent in the wilderness,
so must the Son of Man be lifted up,
and those who look up to Him shall be saved."
You told me so; I believe You, Lord.

Song 3

Days and night He stood for me; He led me, He guarded me.
I will sing, I will dance, I will clap my hands for you, Lord.
I will sing, I will dance, I will raise my voice for you, Lord.
I fell down. He told me to stand up. He led me, I follow;
He cleared the way for me. I am shaken,
He restored me, He stopped me from falling.
I will sing, I will dance, I will clap my hands for you, Lord.
I will sing, I will dance, I will raise my voice for you, Lord.

Christmas Song 1

Christmas time the kingdom of heaven has come to us the atmosphere is calm, quiet peaceful we are experiencing heaven on earth Jesus Christ and his angel are visiting Merry Merry Christmas to you all the spirit of the Lord filled the air everywhere peace, joy, love, harmony happiness, freedom all over the world Merry Merry Christmas to you all we are singing, dancing, praising, celebrating the Lord's birthday Merry Merry Christmas to you all. the Star of Bethlehem has brought joy, peace, harmony, freedom, and love to the world. Sing, smile, dance, jump for the lord and the angels of heaven are watching Merry Merry Christmas to you all. Up alive, happy, healthy, joyful, and lovely. Father, you gave me all things. Jesus Christ of Nazareth, the star of Bethlehem, I am in your care. Watch over me. Father, open my eyes that I can see, stretch my arm that I can reach, lighten my paths from darkness I thank you for the things I did right, and I pray for forgiveness for the things I did wrong. Father, I love you, I thank you, and I pray and ask for your continuous love and mercy that you'll be with me in all my life.

My God and my Lord, I praise you. I glorify your name forever and ever. Amen.

Christmas Song 2

Today is Christmas day our thanks, thoughts, wishes, songs, praises, prayers, loves has risen to heaven Jesus Christ and the angels are watching the entertainment celebrations, they see us, they heard us. Today is Christmas day, the spirit of the Lord is in our midst, they have come to visit us, we felt it, and there is joy peace, love, happiness, calm, satisfaction, free

Prayer

Jesus Christ of Nazareth, the star of Bethlehem,
I am in your care.
Watch over me.
The Lord God from his throne above sees us all,
Moving and walking in great multitude,
Going different directions, doing different things.
Omni-vision, omnipresent,
Jesus Christ of Nazareth, the star of Bethlehem,
I am in your care.
Watch over me.
Lord, from the beginning to the present,
You gave me good health, peace, and joy.
Deliver me from the evil one.
You save me from all dangers.
You heal me from all pains
and from all sickness.
Jesus Christ of Nazareth, the star of Bethlehem,
I am in your care.
Watch over me.
You guard me to my entire destination
and bring me back home safely.
I sleep well and I wake.
Thank you, heavenly Father.
I pray and ask for your continuous mercy.

About the Author

Anthony Agbonkhese wrote this book because the more we know about God, the better life will be for all humans and for all things that the Lord God made and created. He hopes this book will be helpful.

God is a spirit and divine in nature; He made us; we are His children. The earth is His garden, our earthly home, where everything lives and grows; He made it for us to live and keep, tending to enjoy all the great and wonderful things He made and created for us as we learn and journey through our life cycle.

Physically and spiritually, we are together with the Lord God. Joyfully, peacefully, lovingly, and harmoniously, we should relate to ourselves and to others, so His Holy Spirit can lead us and be in control, functioning through us in all His work.

Milton Keynes UK
Ingram Content Group UK Ltd.
UKHW041327301124
451950UK00005B/43